ALSO BY

ERIC-EMMANUEL SCHMITT

The Woman with the Bouquet
Concerto to the Memory of an Angel

THE MOST BEAUTIFUL
BOOK IN THE WORLD
EIGHT NOVELLAS

Eric-Emmanuel Schmitt

THE MOST BEAUTIFUL
BOOK IN THE WORLD
EIGHT NOVELLAS

*Translated from the French
by Alison Anderson*

Europa
editions

Europa Editions
214 West 29th Street
New York NY 10001
www.europaeditions.com
info@europaeditions.com

Translation by Alison Anderson
Original title: *Odette Toulemonde et autres histoires*
Translation copyright © 2009 by Europa Editions

Library of Congress Cataloging in Publication Data is available
ISBN 978-1-933372-74-7

Schmitt, Eric-Emmanuel
The Most Beautiful Book in the World

Book design by Emanuele Ragnisco
www.mekkanografici.com

Cover photo © Laurent Lufroy

Prepress by Plan.ed – Rome

Printed in Canada

CONTENTS

. . . those bouquets of flowers that
set off in search of a heart
and find only a vase.

ROMAIN GARY,
Your Ticket Is No Longer Valid

WANDA WINNIPEG

The leather interior of a Rolls. The leather-clad chauffeur, his leather gloves. Leather suitcases and bags stuffed into the trunk. A woven leather sandal preceding a slender leg slipping out the car door. Of leather is Wanda Winnipeg's scarlet skirt.

The bellboys bow.

Wanda Winnipeg steps over the threshold without looking at anyone or checking to see whether her belongings are following her. How could it be any other way?

Behind the desk at the reception, the employees quiver. Since they cannot be sure of capturing her attention, her gaze invisible behind her dark glasses, they overflow with stock phrases of welcome.

"Welcome, Madame Winnipeg, it is a great honor for us to have you staying at the Royal Emerald. We will do everything in our power to make your stay as pleasant as possible."

She receives these tokens of their high esteem like some small change that is owed her, and does not reply. The employees continue the conversation around her as if she were taking part in it.

"The beauty zone is open from seven in the morning until nine at night, as are the fitness rooms and the swimming pool."

She winces. Panicking, the clerk in charge fears there is a problem.

"Naturally, if you so desire, we can change our opening times and adapt them to your wishes."

The hotel manager arrives hurriedly on the scene, out of breath, slips behind her and gushes, "Madame Winnipeg, what a huge honor it is to have you staying at the Royal Emerald! We will do everything we can to make your time here as pleasant as possible."

Because he has just uttered the same cliché as his staff member, Wanda Winnipeg gives him a mocking smile that she shares with the employees, as if to say, "Not very clever, your boss, can't even express himself any better than you," then she twirls around to hold out her hand for a kiss. The manager fails to notice her derision, and won't even suspect her of it, as she does grant him the grace of a reply.

"I *do* hope I shall not be disappointed: Princess Mathilde has spoken so highly of your establishment."

With a rapid snap of his heels, somewhere between a military salute and a tango dancer's thank-you salute, the manager acknowledges receipt of her command: he is now fully cognizant that accommodating Wanda Winnipeg means accommodating not only one of the greatest fortunes on earth but also a woman who moves in the very highest society.

"Naturally, you are acquainted with Lorenzo Canali?"

With a wave she introduces her lover, a handsome man with long, black, almost polished hair, who nods with a faint smile, perfect in his role as the prince consort who, aware of his inferior rank, knows he must prove more amiable than the queen.

She then moves in the direction of her suite, aware that she leaves murmuring in her wake.

"I thought she'd be taller . . . What a pretty woman! She looks younger than in her photos, no?"

The minute she enters her suite, she can tell she'll feel very much at home here; however, it is with a skeptical pout on her face that she listens to the manager boasting of all its comforts. Despite the size of the rooms, the marble in the two bathrooms, the abundance of bouquets, the quality of the television sets, the precious marquetry on the furniture, she feels that there is something missing, and goes no further than to comment that an extra telephone would be useful for the terrace, should she need to make a call from one of the deck chairs.

"Naturally, Madame, you are right, we will bring it up right away."

She refrains from pointing out that she will never use it, that she will resort to her cell phone, because her intention is to terrorize him until her departure in order to obtain better service. The manager of the Royal Emerald closes the door behind him with a bow, gushingly promising the stars and the moon.

Alone at last, Wanda stretches out on a sofa, leaving Lorenzo and a chambermaid to unpack her clothes. She knows she impresses everyone, and this always amuses her. Because she refrains from giving her opinion, she is respected; because she only ever speaks to give a disagreeable judgment, she is feared. The effervescence occasioned by the briefest appearance is not merely owing to her wealth, or her fame, or her irreproachable looks, but to a sort of legend that surrounds her.

What has she accomplished, after all? According to Wanda, accomplishment can be summed up into two principles: marry well and divorce well.

With each marriage, Wanda climbed a little higher up the rungs of society's ladder. Her last marriage—fifteen years ago—made her what she is today. By tying the knot with the American billionaire Donald Winnipeg, she became famous: magazines the world over published pictures of their wedding. Subsequently she was on the cover for her divorce, one of the juiciest in recent years, with huge media coverage, a divorce that made her into one of the wealthiest women on the planet.

Since then, her life as a woman of independent means has been extremely comfortable: all Wanda Winnipeg has to do is hire very qualified people to manage her affairs; if they prove themselves unworthy, she fires them without a second thought.

Lorenzo comes in, purring in his warm voice, "What's on the program for the afternoon, Wanda?"

"We could have a quick swim in the pool, and then have a rest in the room. What do you think?"

Lorenzo immediately translates Wanda's two orders into his own language: watch her swim her two kilometers, make love to her.

"Fine, Wanda, I like the sound of that."

Wanda sends him a benevolent smile: Lorenzo has no choice in the matter, but it is very elegant of him to play his submissive role with such good grace.

On his way back to the bathroom he sways his hips ever so slightly, so that she can admire his long waist and the curve of the hollow of his back. She muses with voluptuous anticipation that she will soon be able to knead his manly buttocks with her hands.

That's what I like best about them—go figure!

In her inner monologues Wanda uses simple phrases, common formulas that reveal her origins. Fortunately, only she can hear them.

Lorenzo comes back in, dressed in a linen shirt and tight swimming trunks, ready to accompany her to the pool. Wanda has never had such a consummate companion: he never looks at other women, he has no other friends than her own, he eats what she eats, gets up at the same time, and he is constantly in a good mood. It matters little whether he likes everything or nothing: he fulfills his role.

All things considered, he is impeccable. That said, I'm not so bad myself.

She's not referring to her figure, but to her behavior: while Lorenzo may behave as a professional gigolo should, Wanda in turn knows how to treat a gigolo. A few years ago, given Lorenzo's attentive, gallant, irreproachable behavior, she might have had her doubts, might have suspected him of being homosexual. Nowadays it really wouldn't matter if she found out that Lorenzo desired men; it is enough that he fucks her well, and as often as she desires. Nothing else. Nor does she care to know if, like so many others, he slips off in secret to the toilet to inject himself with some substance sure to make him stand to attention before her . . .

We women are so good at pretending . . . Why should it be a problem if they cheat as well?

Wanda Winnipeg has reached that happy stage in the life of an ambitious woman where cynicism finally yields some wisdom: released from any moral compunction, she is free to enjoy life as it is, and men as they are, without becoming indignant.

She checks her date book and reviews the organization of her vacation. Wanda hates to be bored, so she plans everything: charity evenings, visits to villas, meetings with friends, jet-ski outings, massages, restaurant openings, business inaugurations, costume balls; there is very little time left over for spontaneity; time for shopping and siestas has also been predetermined. All of her personnel—Lorenzo included—have a copy of her calendar and have been instructed to oppose any bore who might besiege them with requests for Madame Winnipeg's presence at a dinner or a soirée.

Reassured, she closes her eyes. An odor of mimosas suddenly disturbs her. She feels a sudden dismay, sits up, anxiously inspects her surroundings. False alarm. She is victim of no one but herself. The scent has merely reminded her that she spent part of her childhood here, that in those days she was poor, and her name was not Wanda. No one knows this, nor will they ever know it. She has totally reinvented her biography, and has arranged things so that people will believe she was born near Odessa, in Russia. The accent she has created in five languages—and which so greatly enhances her husky tone of voice—substantiates the myth.

She gets up, shakes her head, banishes memories. Farewell, reminiscence! Wanda controls everything: her body, her behavior, her business, her sexuality, her past. She must have a delightful vacation. Besides, that is what she has paid for.

The week goes by enchantingly.

They flit from "exquisite" dinners to "delightful" luncheons, not forgetting the "divine" soirées. Wherever guests of the jet set are to be found, identical conversations are to be heard and, very quickly, Wanda and Lorenzo are able to join in the discussions as if they had spent their entire summer on the Riviera—talking about the advantages of the Privilege Disco, the return of the string bikini—"such an odd idea, but if you can get away with it, why not"—and that "fabulous" game where you have to convey a film title through mime—"you should have seen Nick, trying to make us guess *Gone with the Wind!*"—and electric cars, "ideal for the beach, darling"—and Aristotle Paropoulos's bankruptcy, and above all that plane crash, the poor Sweetensons' private plane it was—"single-engine, my dear, why on earth have a single-engine when you have the means to pay for a private jet?"

On the last day, an outing on the Farnellis' yacht—"of course you know them, he's the king of the Italian sandal, those very delicate ones with a double lace around the ankle, it's all the rage"—finds Wanda and Lorenzo on the peaceful waters of the Mediterranean.

The women waste no time in grasping the purpose of the outing: to lie on deck in order to exhibit—whatever their age—their perfect figures: firm breasts, narrow waist, legs devoid of any cellulite. Wanda goes along with the exercise with all the natural flair of a woman who knows she has superior good looks and superior grooming. Lorenzo—exemplary, yet again—bathes her in a warm, loving gaze, like a man truly in love. How delightful, no? Wanda garners a few compliments, which put her in a good mood, and it is in this state, enhanced by the rosé wine from Provence, that she follows the merry troupe of multimillionaires onto the beach at les Salins where the Zodiac drops them off.

A table has been set for them in the shade of the restaurant's thatched awning.

"Would you like to see my paintings, ladies and gentlemen? My studio is at the far end of the beach. I'll take you there whenever you like."

Naturally, no one pays the least attention to the humble voice of an old man, and he keeps a respectful distance. Everyone goes on laughing, talking loudly, as if he did not exist. The old man himself thinks he has not made himself heard, so he tries again.

"Would you like to see my paintings, ladies and gentlemen? My studio is at the far end of the beach. I'll take you there whenever you like."

An annoyed silence makes it clear that this time, the bore has been noticed. Guido Farinelli glares at the restaurant owner, who obediently jumps to attention, goes up to the old man, grabs him by the arm and leads him out, reprimanding him.

The conversation starts up again. No one has noticed that Wanda, however, has gone pale.

She has recognized him.

Despite the years, despite the physical deterioration—how old would he be now, eighty?—she trembled on hearing the intonation of his voice.

Hostile, she banishes the memory without further ado. She despises the past. She despises that past in particular, the past she spent in poverty; not for an instant since stepping out on this beach at les Salins has she recalled that she used to come here so often, many years ago, to walk in the sand studded with black rocks—it was a time that all have forgotten, a time when she had not yet become Wanda Winnipeg. Then memory prevails, sharply, in spite of her, against her will and, to her surprise, it brings with it a warm happiness.

She turns discreetly to gaze at the old man; the restaurateur has offered him a pastis. He still looks a bit lost, astonished, like a child who does not understand the world.

Oh, he was never all that smart, even back then. That probably hasn't changed. But he was so handsome!

She found herself blushing. Yes, Wanda Winnipeg, the woman with billions of dollars, can feel something prickly spreading a warmth up her neck and cheeks, just like when she was fifteen years old . . .

Appalled, for a moment she is afraid that the people around her will notice that something is wrong, but instead the discussion, fuelled by the rosé, grows ever livelier.

Behind her smile she decides to give them the slip and, without moving from her chair, protected by her dark glasses, she goes back into her past.

She was fifteen at the time. According to her official biography, at that age she was in Romania, working in a cigarette factory; oddly enough, no one has ever thought to check on that detail, which transformed her, in a very romantic way, into a sort of Carmen who'd managed to get away from her hole. In actual fact, she had been living not far from there, in Fréjus, where a few months earlier she'd been placed in an institution for difficult adolescents, most of them orphans. While she had never known her father, her mother—the real one—was still alive at the time; but the doctors, because of the mother's drug addiction, had preferred to keep her away from her daughter.

Back then Wanda wasn't called Wanda but Magali. A stupid name that she hated. No doubt because no one had ever said it with love in their voice. She had already started using other names. What was it in those days? Wendy? Yes, Wendy, like the heroine in *Peter Pan*. Already on her way toward Wanda . . .

She rejected her name as much as she rejected her family. Both seemed to be a terrible error. At a very young age she already felt that there must have been a mix-up with her identity, they must have made a mistake in the maternity ward: she knew that she was destined for wealth and success, yet here she was, relegated to a rabbit warren on the edge of the highway, with a woman who was poor, slovenly, indifferent, and a junkie. Anger founded on a sense of injustice formed the basis of her character. Everything she experienced from that point on would be a matter for vengeance, a righting of wrongs; she felt she was owed something for such a bungled start in life.

Wanda had already figured out that she would make it on her own. She had no clear picture of what her future might be, but she knew she couldn't count on any diplomas, that her chances had been compromised by such a chaotic education— all the more so that no sooner was she placed in a home for delinquents, subsequent to her shoplifting episodes, than she found herself dealing with teachers whose primary concern was not the subject they were supposed to teach but rather the imposition of their authority—teaching specialists whose mission was to provide not so much an education but an upbringing. So Wanda concluded that it was through men that she would make her way in life. They found her attractive. That much was patently obvious. And she liked the fact that they found her attractive.

Whenever she could, she snuck out of the institution and went to the beach on her bicycle. Open, curious, eager to connect with people, she had managed to establish the notion that she lived not far from there, with her mother. And since she was pretty, people believed her, and they treated her as a local girl.

She wanted to sleep with a man the way other girls her age

wanted to pass a difficult exam: for her, this was the diploma that would put an end to her painful adolescence and allow her to get a start in real life. The only hitch was that she wanted to share the experience with a man, a real one, not a boy her age; already ambitious, she doubted whether a snot-nosed fifteen-year-old could have a lot to teach her.

Every bit as scrupulous and serious in this regard as she would prove to be later in life, Wanda studied the market of available males. In those days, in a territory of five square kilometers, there was one man who stood out: Cesario.

Women had confided in her, and everyone agreed, that he was an accomplished lover. Not only did Cesario—tanned, athletic, slim—have an irreproachable build—all the more visible for the fact that he lived on the beach in his swimming trunks—he also adored women, and was very good at making love to them.

"He does it all, sweetie, everything, as if you were a queen! He'll kiss you all over, he'll lick you all over, and nibble your ears and your buns and even your toes, he'll make you moan with pleasure, he spends hours, he . . . Look, Wendy, in terms of men who are that crazy about women, there's no two ways around it, there's no one else. No one but him. Okay, the only drawback is that he doesn't get attached. He's a bachelor in his soul. Not one of us has managed to hold on to him. To be honest, it's better that way, we can have a go and then, from time to time, have another go. Even when we're married . . . Ah, Cesario . . ."

Wanda would study Cesario as if she were trying to choose a university.

She liked him. Not just because the other women praised his qualities. She really did like him. His skin, smooth and velvety, like melted caramel . . . His green-gold eyes, the whites as pure as mother-of-pearl . . . The blond hair on his body, golden in the sun, as if his body were radiating a luminous aura . . . His torso, slim and rugged . . . And that butt of his, above all, firm, round, fleshy, insolent. Looking at Cesario from behind, Wanda understood for the first time that she was as attracted to a man's butt as a man was to a woman's breasts: a gut attraction, burning inside. When Cesario walked by, his lower body so close to her, it was all she could do not to reach out and touch him, fondle him, stroke him.

Unfortunately, Cesario did not pay much attention to her.

Wanda went with him to his boat, joked around with him, offered him a drink, an ice cream cone, a game of . . . He always took a few seconds to reply, politely, with a hint of irritation.

"That's real sweet of you, Wendy, but I don't need you."

Wanda was furious: he right not need her, but she needed him! The more he resisted her, the more he stimulated her desire: it was going to be him and no one else. She wanted to inaugurate her life as a woman with the best-looking man, no matter how poor; there would be time enough, later, to sleep with ugly rich men.

One night she wrote him a long love letter, full of hope and devotion, and on rereading it, she was filled with such tenderness that she was certain, this time around, of victory. How could he resist such an onslaught of love?

When she came to him, once he had received the message, he was wearing a stern expression and he asked her, coldly, to go with him out onto the dock. They sat facing the sea, their feet dangling near the water.

"Wendy, you're adorable, writing what you did to me. I'm very honored. You seem like a good person to me, very passionate . . ."

"Don't you like me? You think I'm ugly, don't you!"

He burst out laughing.

"Look at this little tigress, ready to pounce! No, you're very beautiful. Too beautiful, even. That's just the problem. I'm not a bastard."

"What's that supposed to mean?"

"You're fifteen years old. You could never tell, that's true, but I know that you're only fifteen. You have to wait—"

"And if I don't want to wait?"

"If you don't want to wait, you can do what you want with whoever you want. But my advice is that you should wait. You mustn't make love just like that, nor with just anybody."

"Well, that's why I chose you!"

Astonished by the young girl's ardor, Cesario looked at her in a new light.

"I'm really shaken up by all this, Wendy, and you can be sure that I'd say yes if you were of age, I swear. It would be yes right away. You wouldn't even have to ask, in fact, I'd be running after you. But as long as you're underage . . ."

Wanda burst into tears, her body shaking with sorrow. Cesario tried timidly to console her, taking care to push her away gently the moment she tried to take advantage of the situation and throw herself at him.

A few days later, Wanda came back to the beach, fortified by their conversation earlier that week: he was attracted to her, and she would have him!

Playing the adolescent who is resigned to her fate, she stopped titillating him or harassing him, and focused rather on taking a psychological angle of attack.

At thirty-eight years of age, Cesario was considered to be what they call, in Provence, a layabout: a good-looking sort who lives off nothing—just the fish he happens to catch—and who wants nothing more than to make the most of the sun, the water, and women, without sparing a thought for the future. But people were mistaken, at least in part, for Cesario did have a passion: he painted. In his wooden hut between the beach and the road, there were dozens of boards—he didn't have the means to buy proper canvases—and tubes of paint, and old brushes. Although no one else thought of him as a painter, in his own eyes he was one. If he failed to marry or start a family, and was happy to have a string of girlfriends, it was not because he was an idler—although that is what everyone believed—but because he wanted to sacrifice himself, devote himself entirely to his vocation as an artist.

Unfortunately, a quick glance was enough to realize that the end result did not justify the effort invested: Cesario produced one lousy painting after another, for he had no imagination, no sense of color, no draftsman's talents. Despite the hours he spent at work, there was no chance he'd ever get better, because his passion was accompanied by a total absence of judgment; he took his qualities for flaws and his flaws for qualities. He raised his clumsiness to the level of a style; and he destroyed the spontaneous balance he could have given to his volumes, on the pretext that such a balance was "too classical."

No one took Cesario's creations seriously: neither the gallery owners, nor collectors, nor the people on the beach, and his various mistresses even less. For him, their indifference was proof of his genius: he must follow his path until he eventually gained recognition—even posthumously.

Wanda had understood as much, and decided to put it to good use. Subsequently she would readily resort to this technique for seducing men, a method which, if properly implemented, is always a success: flattery. In Cesario's case, it wasn't his good looks that wanted complimenting—he didn't care about his looks because he already knew he was good-looking, and could use this to his advantage—you had to be interested in his art.

After devouring a few books she'd borrowed from the institution's library—art history, encyclopedia of painting, biographies of painters—Wanda went back to the beach, well-armed for her discussions. Very quickly, she confirmed his secret belief: he was an *artiste maudit*; just like van Gogh, he would encounter sarcasm on the part of his peers and find glory posthumously; in the meantime he must not doubt his genius for a moment. Wanda got into the habit of keeping him company while he dabbled, and she became an expert on the art of gushing rapturously when she saw his blots and splashes of color.

It moved Cesario to tears to have met Wanda. He could no longer do without her. She incarnated everything he had never dared hope to find: kindred spirit, confidant, impresario, muse. Every day he needed her that little bit more; every day he increasingly overlooked her extreme youth.

And then what was bound to happen did happen: he fell in love. Wanda realized before he did, and slipped into one of her most provocative outfits.

She could tell from his eyes that not touching her was painful to him. Out of a sense of integrity, because he was a decent fellow, he managed to restrain himself, although all of him, body and soul, desired nothing more than to kiss Wanda.

Thus, she could deliver the coup de grâce.

For three days she refrained from going to visit him—he would worry and miss her. On the fourth evening, late at night, she came running into his cabin, tears streaming down her face.

"It's horrible, Cesario! I'm so unhappy! I feel like killing myself."

"What's wrong?"

"My mother has decided—just like that—that we have to move back to Paris. I won't be able to see you anymore."

And everything happened as planned: Cesario took her in his arms to comfort her, she was not consoled, and neither was he; he offered her a drop of alcohol so that she'd feel better; after a few glasses, floods of tears, and an equal amount of rubbing against each other, he could no longer control himself, and they made love.

Wanda relished every instant of that night. The local girls were right: Cesario revered the female body. When he carried her into his bed she felt as if she were a goddess placed upon an altar to be worshipped until dawn.

Naturally she slipped away at daybreak and came back that evening, upset, once again pretending to be desperate. Every night for several weeks an utterly disorientated Cesario tried to console the adolescent girl he loved, first keeping her at a distance and then, after they had brushed against each other once too often, and he had kissed or dried the tears on her eyelashes or under her lips, a distraught Cesario would end up setting aside any moral principles and making love to the young girl with an energy equal to his passion.

Once she knew that she had gained an encyclopedic knowledge of what goes on between a man and a woman in bed—because he did eventually teach her what was pleasing to the man, as well—she vanished.

Back at the institution, she no longer wrote to him, and she perfected the art of sensual delight in the company of a handful of new lovers; then she learned, not without a certain contentment, that her mother had succumbed to an overdose.

A free woman, Wanda ran away to Paris, immersed herself in the city's nightlife and, using men as her support, began her social ascension.

"Shall we go back to the boat or rent some mattresses on the beach? Wanda . . . Wanda! Did you hear me? Shall we go back to the boat or would you prefer to hire some mattresses on the beach?"

Wanda opens her eyes, looks Lorenzo up and down—he seems disconcerted by her absence—and trumpets:

"Why don't we go see those paintings by the local artist?"

"Oh go on, they must be dreadful," exclaims Guido Farinelli.

"Why not? It could be fun!" asserts Lorenzo at once, never missing an opportunity to prove his servility to Wanda.

The troupe of multimillionaires agrees that this might make for an amusing outing, and they follow Wanda, who has approached Cesario.

"Was it you who suggested we come and visit your studio?"

"Yes, Madame."

"Well, could we have a visit just now?"

Old Cesario takes a few moments to react. So used to being rebuffed, he is surprised that anyone might actually speak to him courteously.

While the restaurateur is pulling on his arm to explain to him who the famous Wanda Winnipeg is, and what an honor she is bestowing upon him, Wanda takes her time to examine the ravages of time on someone who was once the most handsome man on the beach. His hair is thin and gray, and he has suffered over the years from too much sun: it has weathered his skin and transformed it into a loose, spotted, leathery hide, with grainy elbows and knees. His squat, thick shape, without a waist, bears no resemblance to the athlete's body he once had. Only his irises have preserved their unusual color of green oyster, although they no longer shine as they once did.

Whereas Wanda has not changed so much; but she has no fear that he might recognize her. Her hair is lighter now, she is hidden by her dark glasses, her voice has become much deeper, her accent is Russian, and above all, there is her fortune— she has thwarted any possibility of identification.

She goes first into the small hut, and straightaway exclaims, "How magnificent!"

She quickly outstrips the entire group: they will not have the chance to see the wretched paintings through their own eyes, they will see them through hers. She grabs hold of each canvas and finds in each a reason to be astonished, to marvel. For half an hour, taciturn Wanda Winnipeg becomes more enthusiastic, talkative, and lyrical than they have ever seen her. Lorenzo cannot believe his ears.

Most astounded of all is Cesario. Mute and gaunt, he wonders how the scene unfolding before his eyes can possibly be real; he is waiting for the cruel laughter or sarcastic remark that will confirm they are merely mocking him for their own amusement.

The rich visitors' exclamations of praise are effusive now: Wanda's admiration has proved contagious.

"It's true, it's original . . ."

"It looks clumsy but in fact it's incredibly masterful."

"The Douanier Rousseau and van Gogh and Rodin must have made a similar impression upon their contemporaries," asserts Wanda. "Well now, let's not waste the gentleman's time any longer: how much?"

"Pardon?"

"How much do you want for this painting? I dream of hanging it in my apartment in New York, on the wall at the foot of my bed to be exact. How much?"

"I don't know . . . a hundred?"

As soon as he says the figure, Cesario immediately regrets it: he's asking too much, he'll see his hopes dashed.

For Wanda, one hundred dollars is the tip she'll leave the hotel concierge tomorrow. For Cesario, it will be enough to pay his debts at the art supply store.

"One hundred thousand?" repeats Wanda. "That seems reasonable. I'll take it."

Cesario has a buzzing in his ears: on the verge of apoplexy, he wonders whether he has heard correctly.

"And this one, would you sell it for the same price? It would go perfectly on the big white wall in Marbella . . . Oh, please . . ."

Mechanically, he nods.

Vainglorious Guido Farinelli, well aware of Wanda's legendary eye for a bargain, and not wanting to be outdone where expense is concerned, sets his heart on another atrocious canvas. When he tries to negotiate the price, Wanda interrupts him, "My dear Guido, I beg you, don't go skimping on the price when you're in the presence of such talent. It's so easy and vulgar to have money, whereas to have talent . . . and such talent . . ."

She turns to Cesario.

"It's destiny! A calling! A mission. It justifies every wretched thing in life."

Calling everyone back to order, she places her checks on the table, makes arrangements for her chauffeur to come fetch the paintings that evening and leaves Cesario dumbfounded, white spittle around the edge of his lips. All his life he has dreamt of just such a moment, and now that it has happened he cannot think of a thing to say, and barely manages not to pass out. He feels like weeping, he would like to keep this beautiful woman here and tell her how hard it has been to keep going through eighty years without an ounce of attention or consideration, he would like to confess to her the hours that he has spent alone at night in tears and telling himself that perhaps he was nothing but a useless wretch after all. Thanks to her, he has been purged of his woes and doubts, he can believe at last that his courage has not been for nothing, and that his stubborn persistence has served a purpose after all.

She holds out her hand.

"Bravo, Monsieur. I am very very honored to have met you."

A FINE RAINY DAY

S he looked sullenly at the rain pounding the Landes forest.

"What nasty weather!"

"You're mistaken, darling."

"What? Just have a look outside. You'll soon see how it's pouring down!"

"Precisely."

He moved onto the terrace, venturing into the garden only as far as the first raindrops and, nostrils flared, ears alert, head thrown back the better to feel the damp breeze on his face, sniffing the mercury sky with his eyes half-closed, he murmured, "It's a fine rainy day."

He seemed to mean it.

That day, she became categorically certain of two things: that he annoyed her, profoundly, and, if she could, she would never leave him.

Hélène could not remember having ever experienced a perfect moment. When she was little, she often surprised her parents with her behavior—constantly tidying her room, changing her clothes the moment there was the slightest spot on them, braiding her hair over and over until she obtained an impeccable symmetry; she shuddered with horror when they took her to see *Swan Lake* because she alone noticed that there was a lack of rigor in the alignment of the dancers, that their tutus did not all drop down together, and that every time there was a ballerina—never the same one—who disrupted the harmony of the movement. At school, she took great care of her things, and if any clumsy oaf happened to return a book of hers dog-eared, she would burst into tears, and by the same token, in her secret consciousness, feel bereft of the frail trust she placed in humanity. As an adolescent she concluded that nature was no better than mankind when she noticed that her two breasts—which were lovely, according to general consensus—were not shaped the same, and that one of her feet obstinately required a size 8 whereas the other was an $8^1/2$, and that her height, despite all her efforts, refused to go beyond five foot seven and one-third inches—five foot seven and a third—is that any sort of a number? As an adult, she dabbled in law studies, going to lectures above all in order to scout for a fiancé.

Not many of the young women had as many affairs as Hélène did. Those who came close to her performance collected lovers because of their sexual appetite or mental instability; with Hélène, on the other hand, it was a matter of idealism. Each new boy seemed, at last, to be the right one; in the stunned delight of their meeting and the thrill of their first times together, she managed to attribute to him the qualities she dreamt of; a few days and nights later, when the illusion had faded and he appeared to her as he actually was, she would abandon him as fiercely as she had charmed him.

Hélène suffered because she was trying to force two mutually repellent requirements to coexist: idealism and lucidity.

At the rate of one Prince Charming a week, she eventually became disgusted with herself and with men. In ten years the naïve and enthusiastic young girl had become a cynical and disenchanted thirtysomething. Fortunately, this had no repercussions on her looks, for her blonde hair continued to ensure her sparkle, her sporty liveliness made her seem cheerful, and her luminous skin retained an eminently kissable pale velvet texture.

When Antoine noticed her at an attorneys' arbitration committee, he was the one who fell in love. She allowed him to pursue an ardent courtship, because he left her totally indifferent. Thirty-five years old, neither handsome nor ugly, pleasant, his hair, eyes, and skin uniformly beige, the only thing that was extraordinary about him was his height: perched up at six foot seven, he would apologize to his classmates for his superior height with a constant smile and a slight hunch of the shoulders. Everyone agreed that his brain was better equipped than most, but no amount of intelligence could impress Hélène, who deemed that she was not lacking therein, either. He showered her with calls, witty letters, bouquets, and invitations to very original parties, and proved himself to be so amusing, so loyal and lively that Hélène, somewhat for a lack of what to do next and largely because she had not yet managed to pin a specimen as gigantic as this one in her herbarium of lovers, allowed him to believe that he had conquered her.

They slept together. The joy it gave Antoine far outweighed any pleasure Hélène may have experienced. She did nevertheless tolerate the continuation of his suit.

Their affair had already lasted several months.

To listen to him, she was the love of his life. When chatting in a restaurant, he could not help but include her in all his plans for the future: as a lawyer he was in demand all over Paris, and he wanted her to be his wife and the mother of his children. Hélène merely smiled and said nothing. Out of respect, or out of fear, he did not oblige her to reply. What were her thoughts?

In fact, she was at a loss to formulate them. To be sure, this affair was lasting longer than usual, but she avoided keeping tally or trying to draw any conclusions. She found him—how could she explain it?—"pleasant," yes, she would not choose a stronger or more affectionate word to describe the sensation that kept her, for the time being, from breaking it off. Since she would be rejecting him anyway, why hurry?

In order to reassure herself, she had established an inventory of all Antoine's faults. Physically, he looked thin, but in reality, was not: with his clothes off, his long body revealed a little baby's tummy that, without a doubt, would prosper in the years to come. Sexually, he made things last, rather than repeating them. Intellectually, although he was brilliant, as demonstrated by his career and his degrees, he did not speak foreign languages nearly as well as she did. Morally, he showed himself to be trusting, naïve to the limits of ingenuousness . . .

However, none of these failings could justify the immediate suspension of their relationship; Hélène was touched by his imperfections. That minimal cushion of fat between his genitals and his navel provided a reassuring oasis on his long bony male body; she enjoyed laying her head there. A drawn-out moment of pleasure, followed by a deep sleep, suited her better now than an incoherent night with a stud and short naps interrupted by brief moments of pleasure. The precaution he exercised in his forays into foreign languages was in proportion to the absolute perfection with which he practiced his native tongue. As for his earnestness, she found it restful; in society, it was always the mediocrity of individuals that Hélène noticed from the very start—their narrow-mindedness, their cowardice, their envy, their insecurity, their fear; no doubt because she was also acquainted with these feelings, she recognized them keenly in others; Antoine, on the other hand, ascribed noble intentions to people—their motives must be worthy, ideal—as if he had never raised the lid on someone's mind to look in and see how it stank and swarmed.

She sidestepped any and all attempts on Antoine's part to introduce her to his parents, and so they had Saturdays and Sundays free to devote to the leisure activities of city-dwellers: cinema, theatre, restaurants, browsing in bookshops and exhibitions.

In May, the opportunity to take four days off work had incited them to go away: Antoine invited her to a villa-hotel in the

Landes, set on the edge of a pine forest by white sand beaches. Hélène was accustomed to family vacations on the Mediterranean; she was looking forward to discovering the ocean and its thundering waves, and to admiring the surfers; she had even planned to go and sunbathe in the nudist dunes . . .

Alas, no sooner had they finished breakfast than the storm that had been brewing was upon them.

"It's a fine rainy day," he said, leaning against the railing overlooking the garden.

While Hélène had the feeling she was suddenly in prison behind the bars of rain, doomed to suffer endless hours of boredom, Antoine was starting his day with an appetite equal to the one he would have had under a brilliant blue sky.

"It's a fine rainy day."

She asked him how on earth a rainy day could be fine: he enumerated all the nuances of colors that the sky and trees and roofs would display when they went on their walk, and the savage might of the ocean, and the umbrella that would keep them close during their walk, and the joy they would feel rushing inside again for a hot cup of tea, and the languor which would ensue, and the opportunity they would have to make love several times over, and the time they would spend beneath the sheets telling each other their life stories, like children safe inside their tent away from the fury of nature . . .

She listened to him. The happiness he felt seemed abstract to her. She did not feel it. However, an abstract happiness is always better than no happiness. She decided to believe him.

That day, she tried to see things the way Antoine saw them.

When they walked through the village, she endeavored to notice the same details he did—the old stone wall, rather than the leaky drainpipe; the charm of the cobblestones rather than their unevenness; the kitsch of the shop windows, rather than their ludicrousness. She did indeed find it hard to wax ecstatic over the potter's craft—fiddling with mud in the 21st century when you could easily buy plastic salad bowls—for it reminded her of the dreadful arts and crafts classes in high school, where she was forced to manufacture old-fashioned presents that no amount of Fathers' and Mothers' Day celebrations could ever suffice to dispose of. She was astonished to learn that Antoine did not find antique stores to be melancholy; he appreciated the value of the objects, whereas for her they gave off a whiff of death.

As they were making their way along the strand, which the wind had not had time to dry between downpours, and she was sinking into sand that was as compact as cement in the process of setting, she could not help but grumble, "The ocean on a rainy day, thanks a lot!"

"But Hélène, what is it you want? The sea, or the sun? Here you have the water, the horizon, all so vast too!"

She admitted that before now she had scarcely ever looked at the sea or at the shore, that she had been quite happy just to enjoy the sun.

"That's an impoverished way of looking at things—reducing entire landscapes to the sun."

She conceded that he was right. Not without a pinch of spite she realized, as she held his arm, that the world was a far richer place for him than for her, because he sought out opportunities to be astonished, and discovered them.

At lunchtime they found a table in an inn which, while elegant, had been designed in a rustic style.

"And it doesn't bother you?"

"What?"

"That it's not authentic—the inn, the furniture, the plates? That the whole décor was designed for customers like you, schmucks like you. High-end tourism it may be, but it's tourism all the same!"

"The place is real, its food is real, and I am really here with you."

His sincerity was disarming. And still she insisted, "So, there's nothing you find offensive here . . ."

He gave a quick, discreet glance all around.

"I find the atmosphere pleasant, and the people are charming."

"The people are horrible!"

"What are you saying? They're perfectly normal."

"Well, look at the waitress, for example. She's terrifying."

"Oh, come on, she's only twenty, she—"

"Yes. Her eyes are too close together. They're tiny and too close together."

"So what? I hadn't noticed. Nor has she, in my opinion, because she seems fairly sure of her charm."

"Good for her, otherwise she'd have grounds for suicide. And look at that one, the wine waiter: he's missing a tooth to one side. Did you notice that I couldn't bear to look at him when he came to take our order?"

"Look, Hélène, you're not going to refuse to communicate with someone just on the grounds that they're missing a tooth?"

"I am."

"Oh, come on, that doesn't make him some subhuman who's unworthy of your respect. You're teasing me, there: humanity has nothing to do with perfect teeth."

When he summed up his remarks in broad generalizations of the kind, she felt it would be awkward to insist.

"What else?" he asked.

"Well, take the guests at the next table, for example."

"What about them?"

"They're old."

"And that's a fault?"

"You want me to be like them! Flabby skin, a bloated tummy, droopy breasts?"

"If you'll only let me, I think I will love you when you're old."

"Stop spouting rubbish. And what about that kid, over there?"

"What? What's the matter with her, the poor kid?"

"She looks like a right brat. And she has no neck. Actually, I suppose you should feel sorry for her . . . just look at her parents."

"What about her parents?"

"The father's wearing a wig and the mother has a goiter!"

He burst out laughing. He didn't believe her, he thought she was picking these details at random with the aim of improvising some sort of entertaining skit. But Hélène really was disgusted by things that, as far as she was concerned, stuck out a mile.

When an eighteen-year-old waiter with flowing hair brought them their coffee, Antoine leaned over to her.

"What about him? He's a good-looking kid. I can't imagine you finding fault with him."

"Can't you see? He has greasy skin, and blackheads on his nose. His pores are enormous—dilated!"

"I imagine all the girls in the neighborhood are after him."

"And what's more, he's the 'clean on the surface' type. Careful! Shaky personal grooming! He'll have athlete's foot. With his type you have to be careful on unwrapping."

"Now there, you are absolutely making things up. I noticed he smelled of aftershave."

"Precisely, that's a very bad sign! Truly clean boys do not drench themselves in perfume." She nearly added, "Believe me, I know what I'm talking about," but refrained from referring to her former life as a collector of men—after all, she did not know how much Antoine was aware of, for fortunately he had been to another university.

He was laughing so hard that she stopped talking.

In the hours that followed, she had the impression she was walking on a tightrope above a void: a single misstep and she would plunge into an abyss of ennui. Several times she sensed the density of that ennui—it was drawing her, begging her to jump, to immerse herself in it; she felt a dizziness, the temptation to jump. So she clung to Antoine's optimism, and he was inexhaustible, with his smile on his face, describing the world to her just as he experienced it. She held tight to his radiant faith.

At the end of the afternoon, back at the villa, they made love for a long time, and he tried so hard to give her pleasure that she repressed her irritation, closed her eyes on all those overwhelming details, and fought to keep up the pretense.

By nightfall she was exhausted. And he did not even suspect the scale of the struggle she had been waging all day long.

Outside, the wind was trying to snap the pines like masts.

In the evening, in the candlelight, beneath the painted beams of a ceiling that was several centuries old, as they were drinking a heady wine, the very name of which had caused him to salivate, he asked, "At the risk of becoming the unhappiest man on earth, I would like your answer to my question: will you consent to be the love of my life?"

She was at the end of her tether.

"You, unhappy? You're incapable of being unhappy. You take everything in your stride."

"I assure you, if you say no, I'll be in a very bad way. I've placed all my hope in you. You alone have the power to make me happy or unhappy."

Basically, it was banal, what he was going on about, the usual blather of a marriage proposal. But coming from him, with his two meters of positive energy and his ninety kilos of flesh always eager for pleasure, it was flattering.

She wondered if happiness might not be contagious. Did she love Antoine? No. He made her feel good about herself, and he amused her. He also annoyed her, with his unshakeable optimism. She suspected that in her heart of hearts she could not stand him, he was so different from her. Does one marry one's closest enemy? Surely not. At the same time, what did someone like her need—someone who woke up every day in a bad mood, who thought that everything was ugly, imperfect, useless? Her opposite. And Antoine, indisputably, was her opposite. While she right not love him, it was patently clear that she needed him. Or someone like him. Did she know anyone else? Yes. Surely. Just now she couldn't think of who it was but she could wait a while still, it would be better to wait. How long? Would others be as patient as he was? And would she have the patience to wait longer, too? Wait for what, anyway? She didn't give a damn about men, hadn't planned on getting married, she had no intentions of producing or raising any offspring. Moreover, the weather didn't seem about to improve from one day to the next, and it would be even more difficult to find a way to escape her ennui.

For all these reasons, she quickly answered, "Yes."

Back in Paris, they announced their engagement and their upcoming wedding. Hélène's closest friends, full of admiration, exclaimed, "How you've changed!"

In the beginning, Hélène did not reply; and then, just to find out how far they would go, she hinted, to encourage them, "Oh yes? Do you think so? Really?"

They would fall in the trap and expand on their comment: "Yes, we would never have believed that a man could have a calming effect on you. Before, no one found favor in your eyes, nothing was good enough for you. Even you yourself. You were merciless. We were convinced that no man, woman, dog, cat, or goldfish would ever manage to keep your interest more than a few minutes."

"Antoine has managed."

"What's his secret?"

"I won't tell you."

"Maybe that's what love is! Just goes to show, one should never despair."

She did not contradict them.

In actual fact, she alone knew that she hadn't changed. She just wasn't saying anything, that's all. To her, life continued to seem ugly, idiotic, imperfect, disappointing, frustrating, unsatisfying; but her judgments no longer passed her lips.

What had Antoine brought her? A muzzle. She showed her teeth less often; she withheld her thoughts.

She knew that she was still incapable of seeing things in a positive light, and she continued to unearth every unforgivable blemish that prevented her from appreciating a human face or restaurant or apartment or performance. Like before, her imagination went on reshaping faces, fixing make-up, adjusting the position of tablecloths, napkins, cutlery, knocking down one wall and putting up another, tossing furniture into the dump, pulling down curtains, replacing the romantic female lead on stage, cutting out the second act, axing the climax of the film; whenever she met any new people, she could, to the same degree as before, detect their stupidity or weaknesses—but she no longer gave voice to her disappointment.

A year after her marriage, which she described as "the most beautiful day of my life," she gave birth to a child whom, when handed to her, she found ugly and flabby. Antoine, however, dubbed the infant "Maxime" and "my love"; she tried very hard to imitate him; and from that moment on, the insufferable little lump of pissing, shitting, and wailing flesh that had ripped her guts open became for several years the object of all her attention. A little Bérénice followed, and right from the start she hated her indecent tuft of hair, yet she continued to behave as a model mother.

Hélène had such difficulty in her own company that she decided to bury her own judgment and, whatever the circumstances, retain only Antoine's view of things. She lived on the surface, his surface, and she kept prisoner inside her a woman who continued to scorn, criticize, vituperate, who pounded on the door of her cell and shouted in vain through the peephole. To ensure herself of the comedy of happiness, she had transformed herself into a prison warder.

Antoine continued to gaze at her with love overflowing; "love of my life," he murmured, stroking her rump or planting kisses on her neck.

"Love of *his* life? Basically, that doesn't amount to much," said the prisoner.

"Well, it's something," replied the warden.

There she was. It wasn't happiness, but the appearance of happiness. Happiness by proxy, happiness by influence.

"An illusion," said the prisoner.

"Shut up," replied the warden.

So it was with a scream that Hélène greeted the news that Antoine had just collapsed along the path.

If she ran so quickly through the garden, it was in order to deny what they were trying to tell her. No, Antoine was not dead. No, Antoine could not have collapsed in the sun. No, Antoine, although he had a weak heart, could not just stop living like that. Aneurysmal rupture? Ridiculous . . . How could anything possibly get the better of a colossus like him? Forty-five years old is no sort of age to go dying. Stupid idiots! Bunch of liars!

And yet, when she threw herself to the ground, she quickly noticed that it was no longer Antoine lying there near the fountain but a corpse. Someone else. A mannequin in flesh and blood. One that looked like Antoine. She could no longer feel the energy he gave off, the electric charge she needed so badly for her sustenance. This was some pale, cold double.

Huddled up, she wept, incapable of saying a word, holding between her fingers those hands, already icy, that had given her so much. The doctor and the medics had to separate the spouses by force.

"We understand, Madame, we understand. Believe us, we do understand."

No. They didn't understand a thing. How could she—who would never have felt like a wife or mother if Antoine had not been there—how could she become a widow? A widow without him? If he disappeared, how would she know how to behave?

At the funeral, she respected none of the proprieties and astounded the crowd of mourners with the violence of her sorrow. Above the grave, before they lowered the body into the earth, she lay on the coffin and clung to it as if to hold it back.

Only upon her parents' insistence, then that of her children—who were fifteen and sixteen—did she consent to letting go.

The box was lowered into the earth.

Hélène walled herself up in silence.

The people around her referred to this state as "her depression." In fact, it was something far worse.

She now had to keep watch over two recluses. Neither one had the right to speak. Behind the wall of silence her desire to keep from thinking was well protected. No more thinking the way she did before Antoine. No more thinking the way she did during Antoine. Each of the two Hélènes had done her stint, and she did not have the strength to invent a third one.

She spoke little, restricted herself to the rituals of hello-thank-you-good night, kept herself clean, wore the same clothes over and over, and waited for nighttime as if for a deliverance, although at that particular time, as sleep evaded her, she was content to sit and work on her crochet in front of the television, paying no attention to either the image or the sound, solely preoccupied with the succession of stitches. Since Antoine had sheltered her from need—money invested, income, houses—it was enough for her to pretend to listen to the family accountant once a month. Her children, once they had finally given up hoping that they might be able to cure or help their mother, followed in the footsteps of their father, and devoted themselves to their brilliant studies.

A few years went by.

Hélène, in appearance, was aging well. She looked after her body—weight, skin, muscles, suppleness—the way one polishes a collection of porcelain figurines in a shop window. When she caught sight of herself in the mirror, she noticed a museum piece, the dignified, sorrowful, well-preserved mother who is occasionally taken out for a family reunion or wedding or baptism, those noisy, chattering, even inquisitorial ceremonies, which she found very trying. As for her silence, she had never faltered in her vigilance. She did not think anything, nor did she say anything. Ever.

One day, in spite of herself, an idea came to her.

What about traveling? Antoine used to adore traveling. Or rather, there was only one thing outside of work that he desired, and that was to travel. Since he had not had the time to fulfill his dream, I could do it in his place . . .

She refused to see what was motivating her: not for a second did she suspect this might be a return to life, or an act of love. If she had thought for an instant that by packing her suitcases she was trying to recover Antoine's kindly gaze upon the world, she would not have allowed herself to continue.

After a brief farewell to Maxime and Bérénice, she began her journey. For Hélène, traveling meant going around the globe from one grand hotel to another. Thus, she stayed in luxurious suites in India, in Russia, in America, and in the Middle East. Every time, she slept and knit in front of a lit screen gabbling in a different language. Every time, she forced herself to sign up for a few excursions, for Antoine would have reproached her had she not done so, but her eyes did not open wide at the sight of what was before her: she would check

whether the postcards displayed in the hotel lobby corre-
sponded to their three-dimensional reality, nothing more . . .
In her seven pale blue morocco-bound cases she carried
around her inability to live. Only when leaving one place for
another, passing through airports, dealing with the complica-
tions of transfers, did she feel a furtive excitement: it was then
that she got the impression that something was about to happen . . . As soon as she reached her destination she was once
again in the world of taxis, porters, doormen, elevator boys,
and chambermaids, and everything was back to normal.

While she may not have acquired an inner life, she did have
an outer life. Moving about, departures, arriving in new places,
discovering new currencies, the need to talk, choosing dinners
in restaurants—there was always a lot going on around her.
Deep inside, everything remained apathetic; her tribulations
had ended up killing off the two recluses; no one was thinking
in her consciousness, neither the sullen woman nor Antoine's
spouse; and it was almost easier this way, this sort of total
death.

These were her circumstances when she arrived in Cape
Town.

She could not help but be impressed: was it the name, Cape
Town, like a promise that one has reached the ends of the
earth? Was it because, as a law student, she had been interested in South Africa's particular tragedy, and had signed peti-
tions calling for equality between blacks and whites? Was it
because Antoine had once expressed a desire to buy an estate
here where they could retire in their old age? She could not
unravel it. In any event, when she found herself on the hotel
terrace overlooking the ocean, she noticed that her heart was
beating fast.

"A Bloody Mary, please."

This, too, surprised her: she never ordered Bloody Marys!
And she couldn't even recall ever liking them.

She stared at the intense gray sky and saw that the clouds, so black with their freight, were about to burst. A storm was threatening.

Not far from there stood a man who was also observing the splendor of the elements.

Hélène felt a tingling in the fleshy part of her cheeks. What was happening? Blood was rushing to her face; a violent throbbing was coursing through the veins in her neck; her heart was beating faster. She had trouble breathing. Was this the onset of a heart attack?

Why not? You have to die someday. Go on, your time has come. It might as well be here. Amidst this sublime landscape. It was meant to end here. This is why, as she was climbing the steps, she had a premonition that something important was about to happen.

For a few seconds Hélène opened her palms, calmed her breath, and prepared to pass away. She closed her eyes, threw her head back, and thought that she was ready: she consented to her death.

Nothing happened.

Not only did she not lose consciousness but, when she opened her eyes again, she was obliged to acknowledge that she felt better. What? You cannot order your body to die? You cannot expire just like that, as easily as you switch off the light?

She turned to look at the man on the terrace.

He was wearing shorts, revealing fine, powerful legs, both muscular and slender. Hélène stared at his feet. How long had it been since she had stared at a man's feet? She had forgotten that it was something she liked, a man's feet, robust limbs that offered so many contradictory qualities—hard at the heel, tender on the toes, smooth above, rough below, so solid that they could carry a big body, so sensitive that they could dread a caress. Her gaze wandered up his calves to his thighs, following the tension and strength hidden beneath his skin, and she caught herself wishing she could touch the blond hairs on his legs, a delicate moss that would be soft under her palm.

Here she had just been all around the world and seen thousands of different types of dress: yet she found that the man next to her was audacious. How dare he exhibit his legs in this way? Weren't his shorts indecent?

She looked more closely and concluded that she was wrong. His shorts were quite normal, she had already seen hundreds of men wearing shorts like those. Whereas he himself . . .

Aware that he was being observed, the man pivoted towards her. He smiled. His face was golden, weathered, marked with deep creases. There was something unquiet in the green of his irises.

Confused, she returned his smile, then absorbed herself in the drama of the ocean. What would he think? That she was trying to pick him up? How dreadful! She could appreciate his expression; his face was sharp, honest, sincere, although his features hinted at a tendency toward sadness. How old was he? Her age. Yes, or something thereabouts, forty-eight . . . Perhaps less, because he was tanned, sporty, with pleasing little wrinkles; he was not the type to smear himself with sun cream.

Suddenly there was a silence; the air stopped humming with insects; then, after four seconds, heavy drops began to fall. A first rumbling of thunder, solemnly confirming the storm's arrival. The light deepened with contrasts, saturating the colors, and moisture rolled over them like the spindrift unleashed on the shore in a tidal wave.

"What filthy weather!" exclaimed the man next to her.

She was astonished to hear herself say, "No, you're mistaken. Not 'What filthy weather' but 'It's a fine rainy day.'"

The man turned to Hélène and examined her closely.

She seemed to mean what she said.

In that split second, he became absolutely certain of two things: that he desired this woman, profoundly, and, if he could, he would never leave her.

THE INTRUDER

This time, she'd really seen her. The woman had gone through the far end of the living room, and had stared at her with an astonished air before disappearing into the shade in the kitchen.

Odile Versini hesitated: should she run after her, or leave the apartment as fast as she could?

Who was this intruder? This was at the third time, at least . . . The previous visitations had been so fleeting that Odile thought her imagination was playing tricks on her, but this time they had actually been able to exchange a glance; it seemed to Odile that the other woman, once she had recovered from her surprise, had winced with fear as she ran off.

Without giving it any further thought, Odile followed her with a shout: "Stop, I've seen you! Don't try to hide, there's no way out!"

Odile rushed into every room—the bedroom, the kitchen, the toilet, the bathroom: no one.

The only place left was the hanging closet at the end of the corridor.

"Come out! Come out or I'll call the police!"

Not a sound from the closet.

"What are you doing in my house? How did you get in?"

Heavy silence.

"Right, I've warned you."

Odile felt a sudden wave of panic: what did this stranger want? She withdrew feverishly to the hallway, grabbed the phone, and after misdialing several times finally managed the number for the police. "Quick, quick," she thought, "that woman is going to pop out of the closet and attack me." Finally, when she had made her way through the barrage of answering machine messages, the beautifully resonant voice of an agent replied: "Paris police, 16th arrondissement, how may I help you?"

"Come to my house, quickly. A woman has gotten in. She's hiding in the closet in the corridor and refuses to come out. Quickly, I beg you, she might be insane, or a murderer. Hurry, I'm very frightened."

The agent took down her name and address then assured her that in five minutes a patrol would be there.

"Hello? Hello? Are you still there?"

"Hmm . . ."

"How do you feel, Madam?"

She didn't reply.

"Stay on the line, don't hang up. There. That way you can let me know if anything happens. Repeat in a loud voice what I've just told you so that this person will hear and know that you're not helpless. Go ahead. Now."

"Yes, you're right, Officer. I'll stay on the line with you, so that this person can't try anything without you knowing about it."

She'd shouted so loudly that she couldn't hear her own voice. Was it distinct? She hoped the intruder, despite the distance, the door, and the coats, had heard what she'd said and become discouraged.

Nothing moved in the dark recesses of the apartment. Such tranquility was more alarming than any amount of noise.

Odile murmured to the policeman, "Are you there?"

"Yes, ma'am, I'll stay right here."

"I . . . I'm feeling a bit panicky."

"Do you have anything to defend yourself with?"

"No, nothing."

"Isn't there some object you could wave that you could use to frighten this person if she gets the wrong idea and starts acting aggressive?"

"No."

"No cane, or hammer, or a statuette? Have a look around."

"Oh, yes, there's my little bronze statue . . ."

"Grab it and pretend it's a weapon."

"I beg your pardon?"

"Call out that now you've got your husband's gun in your hand so you're not afraid of anything. Say it loud."

Odile took a deep breath and bawled in a somewhat hesitant voice, "No, Captain, I'm not afraid because I have my husband's gun."

She sighed, and fought a strong urge to piss on herself: her threat had sounded so feeble, no intruder would ever believe her.

She heard the voice again on the telephone: "Well, how did they react?"

"Nothing."

"Fine. She's frightened. She won't budge until our men get there."

A few seconds later, Odile was speaking to a policeman on the entry phone, then she opened her door and waited for the elevator to bring them up to the tenth floor. Three big sturdy men emerged.

"Over there," she said, "she's hiding in the closet."

Odile shivered when they pulled out their weapons and headed down the corridor. To avoid watching a spectacle that would be devastating for her nerves, she preferred to take refuge in the living room, and from there she heard a vague commotion of threats and orders.

Instinctively, she lit a cigarette and went to stand by the window. Outdoors, although it was early July, the lawns had turned yellow, the trees were losing their reddened leaves. The heat wave had struck the Place du Trocadéro. It had struck all of France. Every day it was fine-tuning its labor of death; every day the evening news lengthened its list of the latest victims: homeless people lying on the burning tar, old people in the hospices dropping like flies, babies expiring from dehydration. And that didn't include all the animals, flowers, vegetables, trees . . . And wasn't that a dead blackbird she could see just down there, on the grass in the square? Stiff as an ink drawing, his feet broken. Pity, blackbirds have such a lovely song.

Consequently, she poured herself a tall glass of water and swallowed it down, just to be on the safe side. True, it was terribly selfish to be thinking of her own welfare when so many others had succumbed, but what else could she do?

"Ma'am, excuse us, ma'am?"

The policemen, at the door to the living room, had trouble rousing her from her meditation on heat wave disasters. She turned around and questioned them: "Well, who was it?"

"There's no one there, ma'am."

"What do you mean, no one there?"

"Come and see."

She followed the three men to the closet. It may have been full of clothes and shoe boxes, but it was empty of any intruders.

"Where is she?"

"Would you like us to have a look around with you?"

"Of course."

With cautious gestures, the policemen went over the hundred and twenty square meters of the apartment with a fine-toothed comb: the interloper was nowhere to be found.

"Really, you must admit that it's rather strange," protested Odile, lighting another cigarette. "She came down the corridor, she saw me, she was surprised, and then she vanished somewhere into the apartment. How could she have gotten out?"

"The rear entrance?"

"It's always locked."

"Let's go see."

They went into the kitchen, and found that the door leading to the back stairs was locked.

"You see," concluded Odile, "she can't have gotten through this way."

"Unless she has a set of keys. Otherwise, how did she get in?"

Odile stumbled. The policemen held her by the arms to help her sit down. She realized they were right: the woman who had burst into her apartment must have a set of keys in order to get in and out.

"It's horrible . . ."

"Could you describe this woman to us?"

"An old woman."

"Sorry?"

"Yes, an old woman. With white hair."

"What was she wearing?"

"I don't remember. Something ordinary."

"A dress, or pants?"

"A dress, I think."

"It doesn't really match the usual profile of a thief or any other kind of ne'er-do-well. Are you sure this person isn't someone you're acquainted with and you just didn't recognize them?"

Odile looked them up and down, somewhat scornfully.

"I understand why you're inferring this, it's logical, given your profession, but do bear in mind that at thirty-five I am neither old nor senile. Undoubtedly I have many more diplomas than you do, I work as a freelance journalist, specializing in geopolitical issues in the Middle East, I speak six languages, and despite the heat I am in absolutely fine form. So please be so good as to believe me when I say that I am not in the habit of forgetting to whom I have entrusted my keys."

Astonished, fearing her anger, they nodded respectfully.

"Excuse me, ma'am, but we have to take every eventuality into consideration. We sometimes have to deal with people who are fragile and who—"

"To be sure, I did lose my calm, there, earlier . . ."

"Do you live here alone?"

"No, I'm married."

"Where is your husband?"

She looked at the policeman with bemused astonishment: she had just realized that no one had asked her this very simple question—where is your husband?—for a very long time.

She smiled. "On a trip to the Middle East. He's a special correspondent."

The policemen showed their respect for Charles's profession with eyes wide open and a concerned silence. The eldest among them did, however, pursue his line of interrogation: "Isn't it possible then that your husband, in fact, could have lent his set of keys to someone who . . ."

"What on earth will you come up with next? He would have told me."

"You can't be sure . . ."

"No, he would have told me."

"Could you call him just to make sure?"

Odile shook her head.

"He doesn't like people trying to reach him when he's halfway round the world. Especially for some nonsense about keys. It's ridiculous."

"Is this the first time something like this has happened?"

"With the old woman? No. It's the third time at least."

"Tell us about it."

"The other times, I just assumed that I wasn't seeing properly, that it wasn't possible. Exactly what you are thinking at this very moment. But this time, I know perfectly well that I wasn't dreaming: I was so frightened! Mind you, I frightened her, too."

"Then I have only one piece of advice to give you, Madame Versini: you must change the keys and the locks immediately. That way you'll be able to sleep in peace. Sooner or later, perhaps when your husband comes home, you'll get to the bottom of this intrusion. In the meantime, at least you'll get a good night's sleep."

Odile nodded, thanked the policemen, and walked them to the door.

Instinctively, she opened a fresh pack of cigarettes, switched the television to her favorite channel, the twenty-four-hour news, then began to think about what to do, approaching the problem from several angles.

After an hour, when she realized that her hypotheses weren't getting anywhere, she picked up the receiver and made an appointment with a locksmith for the following day.

"Two thousand two hundred people have died," announced the anchorman, staring at his viewers. "This summer is proving to lethal."

With her keys in the pocket of her skirt, reassured that nothing would befall her now that she had closed up the house with new locks, Odile succumbed entirely to her fascination with the perverse effects of climate. Streams dried up. Fish stranded. Herds devastated. Farmers in a rage. Water and electricity restrictions. Hospitals overwhelmed. Young interns promoted to physicians. Funeral homes swamped. Gravediggers obliged to interrupt their seaside vacation. Ecologists thundering forth about global warming. She followed each newscast as if it were a new episode in a thrilling soap opera; she was avid for adventure, eager for new catastrophes, almost disappointed when the situation did not get worse. Almost unconsciously, she kept track of the death toll with a sublime delight. The heat wave was a show that did not concern her, but it gave her something to focus on that summer, and distracted her from her boredom.

On her desk there lingered a book and several articles that were waiting to be dealt with. She didn't have the energy to focus on them, at least as long as her editors and publishers were not hounding her, screaming at her over the phone. It was odd she hadn't heard anything, actually . . . Perhaps they, too, were absolutely crushed by the heat? Or dead? As soon as she had the time—or the inclination—she would give them a call.

She surfed the Arabic channels, somewhat peeved that they showed so little interest in the situation in Europe. Truth be told, for them the heat was, well . . .

To ease her conscience she decided to drink a glass of water, and it was while she was headed for the kitchen that she had a strange feeling once again: the intruder was there!

She went back the same direction, had a quick look around. Nothing. And yet it seemed . . . For a split second the old woman's face had appeared to her, no doubt reflected on a lamp or in the angle of a mirror or on the polish of a wardrobe. The image had imprinted itself on her brain.

In the hour that followed she went over her apartment from top to bottom. Then at least ten times over she checked that the old keys could in no way be used to open the new locks. Once she was reassured, she concluded that she had imagined seeing the old woman.

She went back into the living room, switched on the television and it was then, while walking over to her sofa, that she saw her, quite distinctly, in the corridor. Just like the last time, the old woman froze, panicked, and rushed away.

Odile collapsed on the sofa and reached for the nearest telephone. The police promised to come as soon as possible.

This time as she waited Odile did not feel the same emotions as on the day before. Until now her fear had always been quite clearly defined, focused on the old woman in the broom closet and her motivations. But now Odile's fear gave way to terror. She found herself confronted with a mystery: how had the woman gotten back in here today, when the locks had been completely and thoroughly renewed?

The police found her in a state of shock. Since they had already been there the day before, they knew right away what to look for in the apartment.

She was not surprised when they came back to the living room after their search and announced that they hadn't seen anyone.

"It's dreadful," she explained. "The locks were changed this morning, I'm the only person who has a new set of keys, and yet this woman found a way to get in and out again."

They sat down across from her to take notes.

"Ma'am, forgive us for insisting on this point: are you absolutely sure you saw this old woman again?"

"I knew you were going to say that. You don't believe me . . . I wouldn't believe it either if I hadn't experienced it. I cannot blame you for thinking I'm mad . . . I understand only too well . . . No doubt you'll advise me to go and see a psychiatrist—no, no need to protest, that's what I'd say too if I were in your shoes."

"No, ma'am. We're just keeping to the facts. Was the old woman the same one as yesterday?"

"She was dressed differently."

"Does she look like anyone?"

This question confirmed in Odile's mind that the policemen thought this was a matter for a psychiatrist. How could she blame them?

"If you had to describe her, who does she remind you of?"

Odile grew thoughtful: if I confess that she looks vaguely like my mother, they will definitely take me for a nutcase.

"Nobody. I don't know her."

"And what does she want here, in your opinion?"

"I haven't the faintest, I told you I don't know her."

"Why does she frighten you?"

"Listen, dear sir, don't go trying some amateur psycho-analysis with me! You're not a therapist and I'm not a patient. This person is not some projection of my phantasms but an intruder who has been entering my apartment, for what purpose I have no idea."

Because Odile was getting carried away, the policemen murmured some vague excuses, and that is when she had a sudden revelation.

"My rings! Where are my rings!"

She hurried to the dresser next to the television, opened the drawer, and brandished an empty dish.

"They're gone! My rings are gone!"

The policemen's attitude changed instantly. They no longer thought she was deranged, and the case now followed its rational, routine course.

She listed and described her rings, put a value on each one, could not help explaining what was behind each of her husband's gifts, and signed the report.

"When will your husband be back?"

"I don't know. He doesn't keep me informed."

"Will you be all right, ma'am?"

"Yes, don't worry, I'll be all right."

After they had gone, everything seemed banal again, the intruder now reduced to a vulgar thief who worked with disconcerting discretion; but such banality got to Odile's fragile nerves, and she began to cry, loud and long.

"Two thousand seven hundred victims in the heat wave. The government is suspected of hiding the true figures."

Odile was convinced of that, too. According to her own calculations, the number should be higher. That very morning, hadn't she seen, in the gutter in the courtyard, the corpses of two sparrows?

The bell rang.

Since there hadn't been a buzz from the entry phone downstairs, this had to be either a neighbor or her husband. Although her husband had his set of keys, he was in the habit of standing in the hallway and ringing the bell to announce that he was home from his assignment, in order not to startle Odile unduly.

"Dear Lord, if only it were him!"

When she opened the door, she reeled with joy.

"Oh my darling, I'm so pleased to see you! You couldn't have come at a better time."

She threw herself at him and wanted to kiss him on the mouth; however, without actually pushing her away, he continued to hold her in his arms. "He's right," thought Odile, "I'm crazy, getting excited like this."

"How are you? How was your trip? Where were you, already?"

He answered her questions, but she had trouble registering his replies; she also found it difficult to ask the right questions. From two or three dark glances he gave her, followed by a heavy sigh, she understood that she was irritating him somewhat. But she found him so handsome that she couldn't concentrate. The effect of his absence? The more she gazed at him, the more irresistible she found him. Thirty years old, dark, not a single gray hair, his skin bronzed and healthy, his hands long and elegant, his powerful back ending in a narrow waist . . . How fortunate she was!

She decided to unburden herself at once of her bad news.

"We've been burgled."

"What?"

"Yes. My rings have been stolen."

She told him the story. He listened patiently without asking any questions or calling anything in doubt. Odile noted with satisfaction the difference between her husband's reaction and the policemen's. At least he believes me.

When she had finished, he headed for their room.

"Are you going to take a shower?" she asked.

He immediately came back out of the bedroom with a box containing her rings.

"Here they are, your rings."

"What?"

"Yes, all it took was checking in the three or four spots where you usually put them. Hadn't you checked?"

"I thought . . . well, I was sure . . . the last time was in the dresser in the living room . . . next to the television . . . how could I have forgotten?"

"Now, now, don't get angry. Everybody forgets from time to time."

He came over and kissed her on the cheek. Odile's surprise did not dissipate: surprised she had been so silly, surprised that her silliness could elicit Charles's kindness.

She hurried to the kitchen to fix him something to drink, and came back with a tray. And then she noticed that he hadn't left any luggage in the entrance.

"Where's your luggage?"

"Why should I have any luggage?"

"You've just come back from a trip."

"I'm not staying here."

"Pardon?"

"I haven't lived here in long time, or hadn't you noticed?"

Odile put the tray down and leaned against the wall to catch her breath. Why was he speaking to her in such a rough manner? Yes, of course, she had noticed, more or less, that they did not see much of each other, but to go so far as to declare that they no longer lived together . . . What on earth . . .

She dropped to the floor and began to sob. He came over, took her in his arms, and was kind once again: "Come now, don't cry. There's no point in crying. I hate to see you like this."

"What have I done? What did I do wrong? Why don't you love me anymore?"

"Stop this nonsense. You haven't done anything wrong. And I love you very much."

"Really?"

"Really."

"As much as before?"

He took his time to reply, for his eyes were filling with tears while he caressed her hair.

"Perhaps even more than before . . ."

Odile, reassured, stayed like that for a long moment, leaning against his powerful chest.

"I'm going to get going," he said, helping her to get up.

"When will you be back?"

"Tomorrow. Or two days from now. Please don't worry."

"I'm not worried."

Charles left. Odile had a heavy heart: where was he going? And why such a sad expression on his face?

When she came back into the living room, she picked up her bowl full of rings and decided to put it away in the dresser in the bedroom. This time she wouldn't forget.

"Four thousand have died in the heat wave."

No two ways about it, the summer was turning into an exciting one. From her apartment, where she had the air conditioning on non-stop—when was it that Charles had installed it?—Odile followed the news report soap opera as she lit one Virginia cigarette after another.

She had made an arrangement with the concierge, quite a while ago actually, to have her do her shopping. From time to time, in exchange for a few banknotes, the concierge would prepare her meals, for Odile had never been much of a cook. Was this why Charles had drifted away from her? A ridiculous idea . . .

This was the first time he had ever inflicted such a punishment on her: to come back to Paris and stay elsewhere. She struggled to find some reason in their recent past that might justify his behavior, but nothing came to mind.

This was not her only concern: the old woman had come back.

Several times.

It was always the same thing: she appeared suddenly, then vanished.

Odile no longer dared call the police, because of the business with the rings: she would have to confess that she'd found them. To be sure, she could have contacted them, because even though she had made a mistake, she wasn't cheating anyone: after Charles's visit she had tossed the insurance claim form into the garbage . . .

Nevertheless, she sensed that the policemen would no longer believe her.

All the more so in that she had finally discovered what it was that was attracting the intruder—and this, too, was something the police would find hard to believe. The intruder was not dangerous, she was neither a thief nor a criminal, and yet she had shown herself to be a repeat offender often enough to make it amply clear what she was up to: the old lady was breaking in, in order to move things around.

Yes. As odd as that might seem, that was the sole purpose of her surprise visits.

Not only did Odile find the rings that she repeatedly thought had been stolen a few hours later in another room, but the old lady hid them each time in increasingly absurd places, the latest being the freezer compartment in the refrigerator.

"Diamonds at the back of the freezer! What can she be thinking?"

Odile had eventually come to the conclusion that this old lady, even if she was not a criminal, was certainly nasty.

"Or crazy! Completely crazy! Why take so many risks just

to play such an absurd joke? One day I'll catch her red-handed, and then I'll find out."

The bell rang.

"Charles!"

She opened the door and found Charles on the landing.

"Oh, what a joy! Finally!"

"Yes, sorry, I couldn't come back as soon as I had promised."

"Don't worry about it, you're forgiven."

As he came into the apartment, he ushered in a young woman who had been standing behind him.

"You remember Yasmine, don't you?"

Odile did not dare contradict him by admitting that she did not remember the pretty slim brunette who followed him in. It was such a handicap, having no memory for people's physiognomy . . . "Don't panic. It will come back," she thought.

"Of course. Come in."

Yasmine came forward, kissed Odile on the cheeks, and as she embraced her Odile sensed that it mattered little whether she managed to identify this young woman: she despised her in any case.

They went into the living room, and began talking about the heat wave. Odile valiantly took part in the conversation, although her mind could not help but wander from the words they exchanged. "This is absurd, talking about the weather in a worldly way in front of a stranger when Charles and I have so much to say to each other." Suddenly she interrupted the discussion and stared at Charles.

"Tell me, is it children that you're missing?"

"What?"

"Yes. I've been wondering these days what went wrong between us, and it occurred to me that you must have wanted children. As a rule, men don't care as much about having children as women do . . . Would you like children?"

"I have children."

Odile thought she must have misheard.

"What?"

"I have children. Two of them. Jérôme and Hugo."

"I beg your pardon?"

"Jérôme and Hugo."

"How old are they?"

"Two and four."

"Who did you have them with?"

"With Yasmine."

Odile turned toward Yasmine, who gave her a smile. *Odile, wake up, you're having a nightmare, this isn't real.*

"You . . . you . . . you've had two children together?"

"Yes," confirmed the schemer, elegantly crossing her legs, as if it were nothing special.

"And you come into my house, not the least bit bothered, with a smile, to tell me this? You are monsters!"

What happened after that was somewhat confused. Odile's sorrow so upset her that between her cries and her tears she had no idea what people were saying around her. Several times Charles tried to take her in his arms; each time she violently shoved him away.

"Traitor! Traitor! It's all over, you hear, it's finished! Go away! Get out of here, now!"

The more she tried to make him leave, the more he clung to her.

They had to send for a doctor, get Odile to lie down in bed, and force her to take a tranquilizer.

"Twelve thousand victims in the heat wave."

"Good for them!" cried Odile jubilantly to her television screen.

Over the last few days, things had taken a turn for the worse: Charles revealed the ugly side of his nature and ordered her to leave the apartment.

"Never, you hear," she had responded, on the phone. "You will never live here with your slut! These walls are mine by law! And don't try coming around, I won't open the door. Anyway, you don't have the right keys anymore."

At least the intruder had served some purpose! A providential intruder, that old lady.

Thus, Charles rang several times at the door, trying to negotiate his entrance. She refused to listen. Stubborn, he sent for the doctor.

"Odile," declared Dr. Malandier, "you are exhausted. Don't you think a short stay in a convalescent home would do you a world of good? We'd be better able to look after you."

"I can manage perfectly well on my own, thank you very much. To be sure, I'm behind with my articles because of all these problems; however, I do know myself: after a few nights, once I'm better, I'll finish writing them all at once."

"But that's just it, to help you get better, don't you think that a convalescent home . . ."

"These days, Doctor, people are dying in convalescent homes. Because they aren't air-conditioned. Here, it's air-conditioned. Don't you watch the news? There is a heat wave. More devastating than a cyclone. Convalescent home? Despondency home, more like it. Old people's hospice. A house full of dead people. Did he send you here to kill me?"

"Come now, Odile, that's nonsense. And if we find you a nice convalescent home with air-conditioning . . ."

"Yes, where you'll drug me, and turn me into a vegetable, and my husband will take advantage of the situation to confiscate my apartment and come and live here with his old bag! Never! That Arab and her children? Never! Did you have any inkling that he has two children with her?"

"You're really on the verge, Odile . . . a time will come when no one will ask your opinion anymore and you'll have to be taken away by force."

"Well then, you know exactly what I mean, they'll have to take me away by force. Nothing will happen before then. Now go away and don't come back. From now on I shall have a new doctor."

That evening, in a rage, Odile thought of putting an end to her life, and the only thing which stopped her was the idea that that was precisely what her husband and that horrid Yasmine were hoping for.

No, Odile, pull yourself together. After all, you're young . . . how old? Thirty-two or thirty-three . . . oh, I'm always forgetting . . . you have your life ahead of you, you'll meet another man and you'll start a family. That Charles didn't deserve you, so it's better that you found out right away. Just imagine if you'd stubbornly stuck with him all the way to menopause . . .

She suddenly felt an urge to chat with Fanny, her best friend. How long had it been since she'd called her? With this heat wave of a summer, she'd lost her sense of time somewhat. Like everyone else in the country, no doubt she was suffering more than she realized from the sweltering heat, despite the refuge of her shady apartment. She reached for her address book and then flung it aside.

"I don't need to check Fanny's number. If there is one that I do know by heart, it's that one."

She dialed the number and a sleepy voice answered.

"Yes?"

"Excuse me for disturbing you, I'd like to speak to Fanny."

"Fanny?"

"Fanny Desprées. Have I got the wrong number?"

"Fanny is dead, Madam."

"Fanny! When?"

"Ten days ago. Dehydration."

The heat wave! All this time here she'd been sitting there in front of her television adding up the dead and never once had it occurred to her that a friend might be a victim of the carnage. She hung up without adding a word or asking for any details.

Fanny, her sweet Fanny, her old school friend, Fanny who already had two children . . . Two little infants . . . What a tragedy! To die so young, and they'd been born the same year . . . So it wasn't just old people and infants who were succumbing, but also adults in the prime of life . . . Who had answered the phone? She couldn't place that rasping voice . . . an old uncle, someone in the family, no doubt.

Traumatized, Odile swallowed down a bottle of water before going into her room to weep.

"Fifteen thousand dead," announced the anchorman, his face square as an iron door.

"Soon it'll be fifteen thousand and one," sighed Odile, swallowing her cigarette smoke, "for I don't know if I feel much like sticking around in this ugly world."

No sign of temperatures cooling, no storms on the horizon, added the reporter. The earth was cracking with pain.

Nor did there seem to be any way out for Odile. The intruder had been coming several times a day now, up to her clever tricks, mixing up Odile's belongings so that she couldn't find a thing.

Once her concierge had left for Portugal—it is absolutely incredible, the number of concierges there must be in Portugal in August—Odile's shopping and her ready-made meals were brought up to her by the concierge's niece, an insolent girl with a slouch who chewed gum and changed her belt from morning to night, a silly cow you couldn't exchange three coherent sentences with.

Charles had not come around again. No doubt he was the one who was calling when Odile would just say, "No," and immediately hang up. What's more, he was no longer on her mind so much. Hardly at all, in fact. Soon it would be ancient history. Or rather, it was as if it had never happened. Odile's main concern at present was to renew her enrollment at the university but, no doubt because they had people filling in for the summer, she was unable to reach the right person for her re-enrollment. This was extremely irritating.

She really wanted to devote herself to her studies, now. When she wasn't resting in front of the twenty-four-hour news channel, she spent hours at work, reading books about the Middle East, working on her languages, and she seriously intended to finish her dissertation; she'd already started the introduction.

Her dissertation advisor could not be reached. It seemed as if this climatic catastrophe was annihilating the entire country. Nothing functioned normally anymore. Her parents did not answer the phone, either. Everyone must have fled to find a cool spot somewhere.

Well, let's make the most of it and get down to essentials, thought Odile, who spent diligent hours perfecting the structure of her paragraphs or the flow of her sentences. I'll give myself a week to finish this introduction.

She found it so fascinating that she forgot to drink as much as she should. Moreover, her air-conditioning was beginning to malfunction: although she would set the thermostat on 20 degrees, later, after suffering for several hours, she would find it on 30 degrees or 32 or even 15! After a disagreeable search, she located the operating instructions and the warranty, and sent for the technician to come and repair it. He spent half a day working on it and said he didn't understand, maybe there was a bad connection, in any event all the parts had been carefully checked and now it should all work perfectly. And yet the very next morning the meter in each room showed a complete and utterly absurd range of temperatures.

There was no need to call the repairman again because Odile had figured out the origin of the malfunctioning thermo-

stat: the intruder. No doubt the old woman found it delightful-
ly entertaining to modify Odile's settings behind her back.

It did not take long for Odile to begin to feel exhausted—
the work, the heat, the way she would forget to drink—so she
decided to keep a watch out for the intruder, to catch her red-
handed and settle the score once and for all.

When she was certain that she was alone, she huddled in
the broom closet, switched off the light, and waited in ambush.

How long was she on watch? Impossible to say. You'd
have thought the old woman had guessed Odile was waiting
for her . . . After a few hours, with a raging thirst, she emerged
from the closet and went back to the living room. There, God
knows why, she had a sudden urge for a glass of pastis, so she
opened the bar, poured herself a drink and, after one swallow,
something very odd caught her eye.

There was a book on the shelf that bore her name: Odile
Versini, inscribed on the spine. After she pulled it from the
shelf, she stood there completely baffled by the cover: this was
her dissertation, the dissertation she was in the process of writing. And here it was in full—finished, printed on four hundred
pages, published by a prestigious house she could never have
dreamed of approaching.

Who was playing these practical jokes on her?

She leafed through the opening pages and went pale. Here
were the premises of her introduction—the one she'd been
slaving over for days—but it was finished, better written, with
far greater mastery.

What was going on?

On raising her eyes, she saw the intruder. The old lady was
looking her up and down, quite calmly.

No. This time, enough was enough.

She hurried back the way she had come, to the broom closet, grabbed the golf club she'd already singled out as a weapon,
and came back to have it out with her intruder once and for all.

*

By the window which overlooked the gardens of the Trocadéro, Yasmine was contemplating the rain which had come
to reconcile the earth with the sky and put an end to the epi-
demic of death.

Behind her, the room was unchanged; it was still overflowing with books, a precious collection for anyone interested in
the Middle East. Neither she nor her husband had had time to
change the décor or the furniture. They would start the reno-
vations later on; they had not hesitated to leave their tiny apartment on the ring road, where they had been living in cramped
quarters with their two children, in order to move in here.

And there they were, Jérôme and Hugo, right behind her,
discovering the pleasures of satellite television; they could not
stop channel-surfing.

"It's great, Mom, they have Arabic channels!"

They never stopped to watch one program; what intoxicated them was the idea of having so many programs, rather than
being tempted by just one of them.

Her husband came in and slipped behind her, kissing the
base of her neck. Yasmine turned around, pressed against him.
They put their arms around each other.

"Do you know I had a look through your family album: it's
incredible how much you look like your father."

"Don't say that."

"Why? Because he died in Egypt when you were only six? I
understand that it makes you sad—"

"No, it's not that. I'm sorry because it makes me think of
Mother. She often mistook me for him, she called me Charles."

"Don't think about it anymore. Remember your mother as
she was when she was in good health—a brilliant intellectual,
full of wit and clever conversation—she always made a great
impression on me. Forget these last two years."

"You're right. Alone in this place, with the disease, she didn't even recognize her own self. With her memory fading like that, she grew younger; she thought the old woman she saw in the mirror was an intruder. The way they found her with her golf club by the broken mirror. I guess she wanted to threaten the intruder, to defend herself when she thought the other woman was about to strike her."

"We'll go to see her on Sunday."

Yasmine stroked François's cheeks and added, drawing closer with her lips, "It's not so hard now that she's gone back to the period before your father. She doesn't mix us up anymore. How old do you suppose she thinks she is?"

He let his head fall against Yasmine's shoulder.

"There are times when I wish that the day my mother becomes a newborn baby would arrive soon, so I can take her in my arms. At last I'll be able to tell her how much I love her. For me, a kiss farewell. For her, a welcome . . ."

THE FORGERY

You might say that there were two Aimée Favarts. Aimée before the separation. And Aimée afterwards.

When Georges told her that he was leaving her, it took Aimée several minutes before she could be sure that this was neither a nightmare nor a joke. Was this truly Georges speaking? And was it really her that he was speaking to? Once she was forced to admit that reality was indeed dealing her this blow, she took the trouble to make sure she was still alive. This diagnosis took somewhat longer to establish: her heart had stopped beating, her blood had stopped flowing, a silence cold as marble had petrified her organs, a stiffness prevented her eyelids from blinking . . . But Georges was still perfectly audible ("You understand, my darling, I can't go on any longer, everything has to come to an end sometime") and visible (rings of sweat dampened his shirt around his armpits), and she could smell him, that scent that made her head spin, a male smell of soap and fresh lavender-scented laundry . . . Astonished, almost disappointed, she concluded that she had survived.

Gentle, urgent, cordial, Georges said one thing after another in order to fulfill two contradictory requirements: announce that he was leaving her, and make it seem as if it were not such a serious thing.

"We've been happy together. I owe my moments of greatest happiness to you. I am sure that when I die I'll be thinking of you. But I am the head of the household. Could you have loved me if I'd been one of those men who sneak off, who shirk their responsibilities—wife, home, children, grandchildren—with a snap of the fingers?"

She felt like screaming, Yes, I would have loved you, it's even what I've wanted from the very first day, and yet, as usual, she did not say a thing. Not to hurt him. Above all, not to hurt him. To Aimée, Georges's happiness seemed so much more important than her own: this is how she had loved him for twenty-five years, forgetting herself.

Georges went on: "My wife has always assumed we would spend the rest of our lives in the South of France. Since I'll be taking my retirement two months from now, we've bought a villa in Cannes. We move this summer."

More than the departure itself, it was the expression "spend the rest of our lives" which Aimée found shocking. While to his mistress he had always portrayed his family life as nothing less than a prison, she was now discovering with this "spend the rest of our lives" that Georges, in another world to which he had never given her access, had continued to feel like a husband to his wife and a father to his children.

"Our lives!" Aimée had been nothing more than an interlude. "Our lives!" No matter how often he had whispered words of love to her, or how often his body had called out for hers, she remained a passing fancy. "Our lives!" In the end, the other woman—the rival, so feared, despised—had won! Did she even know? Was she aware, as she settled with her husband in Cannes, that in her wake she was leaving a woman—stunned, battered—who for twenty-five years had dreamt of taking her place, and who had still been dreaming of it not even five minutes ago?

"Answer me, darling, say something, at least . . ."

She stared at him and her eyes got bigger and bigger. What? He's on his knees? He's rubbing my hand? What is he up to now? No doubt he's going to start crying any minute . . . He always sobs before I do . . . It's irritating, I've never been able to make him yield to my tenderness because I've always had to console him first. A very useful trick, this behaving like a man when it's called for, and like a woman when the mood takes him.

She looked closely at the sixty-something man who was there at her feet, and suddenly felt that he was a total stranger. If the rational part of her brain hadn't whispered to her that this was Georges, the man she'd been worshipping for twenty-five years, she would have got to her feet with a shout: "Who are you? What are you doing in my house? And who gave you permission to touch me?"

It was at that moment, the very moment when she believed he had changed, that she changed. Looking down at that maggot with his dyed hair sobbing like a baby and drooling all over her knees and her hands, Aimée Favart was transformed into a new Aimée Favart. The one from afterwards. The one who no longer believed in love.

In the months which followed, there was, to be sure, some coming and going between the old Aimée and the new Aimée: after a half-hearted suicide attempt, she slept with Georges again one night; by August, however, when he had moved, the new Aimée was in full possession of the old one. Better still: she had killed her.

She thought back on her past with amazement.

How could I ever have believed he loved me? He just wanted a mistress who was beautiful, nice, and stupid.

Beautiful, nice, and stupid . . .

Beautiful—that, Aimée definitely was. Up until their separation, everyone had dwelled on her beauty. Except for Aimée herself. Because, like many women, Aimée had not been allotted the beauty that she admired. She was petite, and slim, with small breasts, but she envied big curvaceous women, she developed a complex because she was short and slim. After her separation she learned to appreciate herself the way she was, and she concluded that she was "far too good for just any man."

Nice—Aimée was nice because she underestimated herself. She was the only daughter of a mother who had never revealed her father's identity to her, treating her like some sort of burdensome reproach, hence she knew nothing about the world of men. Thus, when she started work as a secretary in the firm Georges managed, she did not know how to resist an older man who, in her candid virgin's eyes, incarnated both a father and a lover. And where would the romantic element come in? It seemed more noble to her to love a man whom she could not marry . . .

Stupid? In Aimée, as in every human being, stupidity and intelligence resided in separate provinces, which made her regionally brilliant but locally stupid: while she proved to be perfectly competent in the realm of work, she was an utter ninny when it came to emotions. A hundred times or more her colleagues had advised her to break up with that man; a hundred times or more she reveled in the voluptuous delight of not listening to them. So they spoke for the voice of reason? She prided herself in speaking for the heart.

For twenty-five years, she and Georges shared the everyday routine of work, but none of the everyday routine of conjugal life. This made their escapades seem all the more beautiful, all the more precious. There were the hastily stolen caresses at work, and she only ever received him at her home under the rare pretext of an interminable board meeting. In twenty-five years, their relationship never had time to grow shopworn.

Three months after he moved to the South of France, Georges began writing to Aimée. With each passing week his letters became more ardent, more passionate. Was this the effect of absence?

She did not reply. For, while his correspondence may have

been addressed to the old Aimée, it was the new Aimée who read them. Without emotion she inferred that Georges must already be feeling bored with his wife. Scornfully, she read through the pages that embellished their past together, each time a bit more.

He's gone mad in his retirement! At this rate, three months from now we'll have lived in Verona and our names will be Romeo and Juliet.

She stayed on at her job, found the new director to be a ridiculous man—especially when he smiled at her—and took up sports with a vengeance. She was forty-eight years old and she'd been forbidden from the start from having children, because Georges already had his own; now she was determined not to regret her lack of offspring.

"Just so that they can steal my best years, suck my heart dry and then disappear one day, leaving me even more alone? No, thanks. And besides, to go and add more people to a planet already rotten with overpopulation and human stupidity, you have to be either completely stupid or completely oblivious."

Her firm was going through a rough time, and Monsieur Georges, the former director, was sorely missed. There was some restructuring, a redundancy scheme, and at the age of fifty, Aimée Favart, not really all that surprised, found herself unemployed.

Drifting from useless internships to infantilizing training programs, she looked half-heartedly for a new job, and in the meanwhile she ran into financial difficulties. She felt no nostalgia as she took her jewelry box to a secondhand dealer.

"How much did you hope to get for all this, Madame?"

"I've no idea . . . I'm counting on you to tell me."

"It's just that . . . there's nothing of any value here. It's all costume jewelry, there are no precious stones, no solid gold, nothing that . . ."

"That doesn't surprise me in the least. It was he who gave them to me."

"He, who?"

"The man who said he was the love of my life. He gave me cheap junk, just like the stuff the Spanish conquistadors gave the Indians in America. And you know what? I was such a lump that I liked it. So everything's worthless?"

"Pretty much so."

"What a bastard, don't you think?"

"I wouldn't know, Madame. It's true that when you love a woman . . ."

"Well?"

"When you love a woman, you don't spend your money on jewelry like this."

"Ah! You see? I was sure of it."

She felt triumphant. The jeweller, on the other hand, had merely resorted to a phrase he was accustomed to using in a rather different situation: when he wanted to convince a customer to buy a more expensive item.

Although she left the shop with only three meager banknotes, her heart was full of joy: a specialist had confirmed that Georges was nothing but a filthy bastard.

As soon as she got home, she opened her cupboards and started hunting down all the gifts she'd ever received from Georges. Not only did the loot turn out to be fairly insubstantial in quantity, but the quality was laughable. A rabbit-skin coat. Nylon underwear. A watch no bigger than an aspirin tablet. A leather notebook of no particular brand that still smelt of goat. Cotton underwear. A hat that you couldn't possibly wear anywhere, except perhaps at an English royal wedding. A silk scarf with the label snipped off. Black rubber underwear.

Flopping onto her bed, she didn't know whether to laugh or to cry. She made do with a cough. Here were her trophies for twenty-five years of passion! Her war booty . . .

In order to feel less wretched, she turned her scorn against him. He had always used the pretext that he could not risk arousing his wife's suspicions with regular, unjustified expenses, therefore he had not exactly been generous with her. Generous—what am I saying? Normal. Not even normal. A skinflint, that's what he was!

And here was I, basking in glory! Priding myself on the fact that I didn't love him for his money! What a dolt! I thought I was exalting the lover, I was merely flattering the miser . . .

As Aimée went into the living room to feed her parakeets and paused by the painting that hung above their cage, she nearly choked with rage.

"My Picasso! That really is the proof that he took me for a fool!"

The canvas, its forms playfully dispersed—the puzzle of a face, an eye here, the nose just above, an ear in the middle of the forehead—was supposed to represent a woman with her child. Had Georges not behaved very oddly the day he brought it to her? Pale, his lips waxy, his voice breathless, he was trembling when handed the canvas to her.

"Right, this time I've made up for all the other times. No one can dispute the fact that at least this once I have been generous with you."

"What is it?"

"A Picasso."

She'd removed the protective cloths, and now she contemplated the work and said again, as if to convince herself, "A Picasso?"

"Yes."

"A real one?"

"Yes."

Hardly daring to touch it, for fear that some clumsy gesture might cause it to disappear, she had stammered, "How is this possible? How did you manage it?"

"Oh, I beg you, don't ask me that, ever!"

At the time, she had taken his reserve for the modesty of a man who had bled himself dry in order to offer something to a woman. Later, when she thought back on his terrified behavior, she succumbed to a brief moment of delirium and wondered whether he hadn't stolen it. And yet he seemed so proud of his gift . . . And he was an honest man.

For her protection, he had advised her to assert that the painting was a forgery.

"You see, my darling, it is highly unlikely that a little secretary living in low-income housing would own a Picasso. People will make fun of you."

"You're right."

"Worse than that, if anyone ever did suspect the truth, you would be burgled for sure. Your best insurance, believe me, is to insist, for as long as you don't part with the painting, that it is a forgery."

So Aimée had shown the painting to the rare visitors who came to her apartment as "My Picasso—a forgery, of course," accentuating the joke with a burst of laughter.

With hindsight, Georges's trick seemed diabolical: to oblige her to insinuate that her Picasso was a forgery so that she, and she alone, would be convinced that it was authentic!

Still, in the weeks which followed, her feelings were ambiguous: on the one hand she was sure she'd been had, and on the other she still hoped she might be mistaken. Whatever she might learn about her canvas, she would be disappointed. Disappointed to find out she was poor, or disappointed to have to find some qualities in Georges after all.

She fell to standing there beneath the frame, and it became the ring where the old Aimée and the new Aimée would thrash it out—the former who had believed in love and the authentic Picasso, and the latter who saw everything fake there was about Georges and the painting.

As her unemployment benefits dwindled, Aimée struggled to find a new job. When she went in for job interviews, she made no effort to put her best side forward, as it was so important to her now not to be taken in: the human resources people saw before them a hard, brittle, uncommunicative woman, her lack of qualifications compounded by her age, her financial requirements, and a difficult character that was incapable of compromise, quick to suspect that she would be exploited, and so very defensive that she seemed aggressive. Without realizing it, she had disqualified herself from the race she was supposed to be running.

When she had scraped up her last savings, she realized that if she did not do something right away she would be officially poverty-stricken. Instinctively, she hurried over to her desk, hunted feverishly through the drawer in search of an old scrap of paper where she had jotted down the number, and called Cannes.

A cleaning woman answered, took note of her request, and vanished into the silence of a spacious residence. Then Aimée heard footsteps and recognized Georges's short, anxious breathing.

"Aimée?"

"Yes."

"Well, what is going on? You know very well you can't call me at my wife's."

In a few short sentences, without difficulty, she sketched out an apocalyptic picture of her situation. It would not have taken much for her to feel sorry for herself, but her new armor of cynicism prevented her from any effusions of self-pity, and hearing Georges's anxious breathing on the line filled her with a sort of rage.

"Georges, I beg you, help me," she concluded.

"Just sell the Picasso."

She thought she had misheard. What? He dared to . . .

"Yes, my sweet, all you need to do is sell your Picasso. That's why I offered it to you. To keep you sheltered from want, since I couldn't offer marriage to you. Go and sell the Picasso."

She closed her mouth to keep from screaming. So, right to the end, he was going to take her for a fool!

"Go to Tanaev on the rue de Lisbonne, at number 21. That's where I bought it. Make sure they don't rip you off. Ask for Tanaev the father. Oh, oh, I have to hang up. My wife is coming. Good bye, my dear Aimée, I think about you all the time."

He had already hung up. Evasive coward. Just what he'd always been.

What a slap in the face! Served her right. She shouldn't have called him in the first place.

Humiliated, Aimée stood beneath the picture and unleashed her fury.

"Never, do you hear me, never will I go to some art dealer just to be told that I'm stupid and Georges was a bastard—I already know that, thank you very much!"

Two days later, however, with the electricity company threatening to switch off the power, she got into a taxi and said, "Tanaev, at 21, rue de Lisbonne, please."

Although at that address she saw nothing but a children's clothing store, she nevertheless got out of the taxi, with her painting in its wrapping tucked under her arm, and went over to the building.

"He must work upstairs or at the back."

She read four times over the list of residents on either side of the entryway, then hunted for a concierge who could give her Tanaev's new address, but eventually realized that these buildings for rich people, unlike those of the poor, resorted to anonymous cleaning services.

Before giving up and heading back home, she entered the clothing store for good measure.

"Excuse me, I'm looking for Mr. Tanaev, the father, and I thought that . . ."

"Tanaev? He moved away ten years ago."

"Ah, do you know where he moved to?"

"Move? People like him don't move, they vanish. Period."

"Whatever do you mean?"

"Once they've got their pile, they have to go and hide it somewhere. God knows where he is now—Russia, Switzerland, Argentina, Bermuda . . ."

"It's just that . . . you see . . . he sold me this painting some years ago . . ."

"Oh, you poor woman!"

"Poor, why?"

The shopkeeper saw that Aimée had gone extremely pale, and he was sorry he had spoken so quickly.

"Listen, my dear lady, I'm no expert. Maybe your painting is absolutely superb, and it's surely worth a fortune. Here, let me give you something . . ."

He hunted for a card in a box where he had a lot of loose papers.

"Here. Go to see Marcel de Blaminth, rue de Flandres. Now *he's* an expert."

When she went through the door at Marcel de Blaminth's, Aimée lost all hope. Heavy drapings of crimson velvet absorbed external noise or influence, and monumental canvases in tortured gilded frames made Aimée instantly, crushingly, aware that she was no longer in the known world.

An imperious secretary with a tight chignon gave her a suspicious look from behind her tortoiseshell glasses. Aimée mumbled her story, pointed at her painting, and the battleaxe led her to the inner office.

Marcel de Blaminth studied his visitor in detail before looking at the painting. Aimée had the impression she was being judged from head to toe, that he was evaluating the price and origin of every single item of clothing or jewelry she had on her. As for the canvas, he only gave it a cursory look.

"Where are the certificates?"

"I don't have any."

"Deed of sale?"

"It was a gift."

"Could you get it?"

"I don't think so. The . . . the person has vanished from my life."

"I see. Perhaps we could get it from the dealer? Who was it?"

"Tanaev," murmured Aimée, almost ashamed.

He raised an eyebrow and his eye beamed with sumptuous disdain.

"This does not augur well, Madame."

"Couldn't you perhaps . . ."

"Have a look at the painting? You are right. That is what matters. Sometimes some very fine work ends up here after a very obscure or checkered past. It is the work that counts, nothing but the work."

He changed his glasses and drew nearer to the Picasso. His analysis was thorough. He studied the canvas, felt the frame, measured it, observed details with a magnifying glass, stepped back, started all over.

Finally, he put his palms on the table.

"I won't ask you to pay for the consultation."

"No?"

"No. It would be pointless to heap misfortune upon misfortune. It is a forgery."

"A forgery?"

"A forgery."

To save face, she burst out laughing, "That's what I've always told everyone."

Back at home, Aimée hung her picture back on the wall above the parakeets' cage, and forced herself to be lucid, an ordeal which few human beings are ever called upon to undergo. She counted her shipwrecks: her inner life, her family life, her professional life. Looking at herself in the full-length mirror in her bedroom, she found that her figure, sculpted by exercise and a macrobiotic diet, was holding up well. For how much longer? In any case, however proud she might be of her body now, it would go no further than the mirror on her wardrobe: she did not want to give it to anyone.

She went into the bathroom with the firm intention of lazing in her tub, and the vague idea of committing suicide.

Why not? It may be the solution. What sort of future do I have left? No work, no money, no man, no children, and nothing to look forward to but old age and death. A fine program . . . the logical choice is to kill myself.

But logic alone was pointing to suicide; she didn't feel like dying. Her skin craved the warmth of the bath; her mouth watered at the thought of the melon and the thin slices of ham waiting on the kitchen table; her hand checked the irreproachable smooth curves of her thighs and strayed up to her hair, to linger in its silken vigor. She let the water run and tossed in an effervescent tablet that released a perfume of eucalyptus.

What could she do? Go on surviving?

The concierge rang at the door.

"Madame Favart, would it help you out to rent your guest room?"

"I don't have a guest room."

"Yes you do, the little room which overlooks the stadium."

"That's where I do my sewing and my ironing."

"Well, if you put a bed back in there, you could rent it out to students. Since the university is right nearby, they're always coming and asking me if there are any rooms to rent around here . . . You could supplement your income, until you find a new job, which I'm sure won't be long, in any case."

As she stepped into her bath, quite moved, Aimée felt

obliged to thank God, in whom she did not believe, for having sent a solution to her problem.

For the next ten years, she rented her guest room to young women studying at the neighboring university. This additional income, added to the bare minimum she got from the state, was enough for her to get by while she waited for retirement. Given the fact that housing tenants had become her true profession, she would only select them after careful review, and could easily have composed the six commandments of the wise landlady:

1. Demand one month's rent in advance, and have all the exact contact information for the parents.

2. Up to the very last day, behave toward the tenant the way a hostess would behave toward a gatecrasher at her party.

3. Prefer older sisters to younger ones: they are invariably more docile.

4. Prefer petit-bourgeois girls to rich ones: they are generally cleaner and less insolent.

5. Never let them talk to you about their private life, for if you do they'll end up bringing boys over.

6. Prefer Asian girls to European ones: they are more polite, more discreet, might show some gratitude, and they even bring you presents.

Although Aimée never became attached to any of her tenants, she did appreciate not living alone. A few words exchanged each day were enough, and she loved to make these silly young geese aware that she had more experience than they did.

Life might have continued along like this for a long time if the doctor had not detected some suspicious growths: cancer had spread throughout Aimée's body. This news—which she intuited more than she received—made her feel as if a burden had been lifted: no more struggle to survive. Her only dilemma: did she still need to rent the room that winter?

It was October, and she had just taken on, for the second year in a row, a young Japanese girl, Kumiko, who was finishing her degree in chemistry.

She confided in the discreet student:

"Here's the thing, Kumiko: I have a very serious illness which will mean that I'll have to spend a lot of time in the hospital. I don't think I'll be able to go on lodging you."

The young girl's sorrow was such a surprise that initially she misunderstood the cause, attributing the young foreigner's tears to the fear she must have of being left out in the street; but Aimée did eventually concede that Kumiko was truly sorry to see what was happening to her landlady.

"I help you. I come see you in hospital. I can cook good food. Take care of you. Maybe I go take room in dormitory, still I find time for you."

Poor girl, thought Aimée, at her age I was just as kind and naïve. When she'll have been through as much as I have, she'll sing a different tune.

Both burdened and disarmed by the girl's displays of affection, Aimée did not have the heart to send Kumiko away, so she continued to rent the room to her.

It was not long before Aimée was admitted into the hospital on a permanent basis.

Kumiko came to visit her every evening. Her only visitor.

Aimée was not used to receiving so much care and attention; there were days when she appreciated Kumiko's smile, like a balm enabling her to believe that humanity was not so rotten after all; there were other days when, as soon as she saw the Japanese girl's kindly face, she rebelled against this intrusion into her dying days. Could she not be left to die in peace? Kumiko ascribed Aimée's moods to the progression of the disease; so, despite the rebuffs, despite the insults and bursts of anger, she forgave the bedridden woman and remained steadfast in her compassion.

One evening the Japanese girl committed an error that she was not aware of, and which altered Aimée's entire behavior. The doctor had confessed to his patient that the new treatment was disappointing. Translation? You haven't got much longer. Aimée did not bat an eyelash. She felt a sort of cowardly relief, of the kind an armistice might offer. No more need to fight. No more exhausting therapy on the horizon. The torture of hope—and its attendant disquiet—would finally be removed. All that was left was to die. So it was with a sort of serenity that Aimée informed Kumiko that the new therapy had failed. But the Japanese girl reacted with passion. Tears. Cries. Hugs. Screams. Calm. Tears again. When finally she was able to speak, Kumiko grabbed her cell phone and called three people in Japan; half an hour later she announced triumphantly to Aimée that if she were to go there, to Kumiko's island, she would be able to obtain a treatment that was not yet available in France.

Lifeless, exhausted after submitting to Kumiko's demonstration of affection, Aimée waited for the young woman to leave. How dare this youngster spoil her death! How dare she torment her further with talk of cures?

Aimée decided to seek revenge.

The next day, when Kumiko showed her face at the hospital, Aimée spread her arms and called her over.

"My little Kumiko, come and give me a hug."

After a few sobs and just as many tender hugs, Aimée poured forth—her tone pathetic and punctuated with sighs—a long declaration of love, according to which Kumiko had become a daughter to her, in her eyes, yes, the daughter she had never had and that she had always dreamt of having, the daughter who was by her side in her final hours and who made her feel that she was not alone in the world.

"Oh my friend, my dear young friend, my great friend, my only friend . . ."

She so excelled at varying the motif that she ended up feeling moved herself, pretending less and expressing herself more.

"You are such a good girl, Kumiko, good in the way I was at your age, when I was twenty, when I believed in human honesty, in love, in friendship. You are as naïve as I was, my poor Kumiko, and no doubt some day you will be as disappointed as I have been. I feel sorry for you, my dear, you know. But what does it matter? Hold fast, stay as you are for as long as possible. There will be time enough for disappointment and betrayal."

Suddenly she took hold of herself and remembered her plan. Revenge. So she continued, "To reward you, and enable you to believe in human goodness, I have a present for you."

"No, I don't want."

"Yes, I am going to leave to you the only thing of value that I possess."

"No, Madame Favart, no."

"Yes, I am leaving you my Picasso."

The young girl stood with her mouth gaping.

"You have noticed the painting above the parakeet cage— well, it's a Picasso. A real Picasso. I tell everyone it's a copy so that I won't have problems with envy or burglars; but you can believe me, Kumiko, it's a real Picasso."

Petrified, the young girl went pale.

Aimée shivered for a second. Does she believe me? Might she suspect it's a simulacrum? Does she know anything about art?

Tears gushed from the girl's slanting eyes, and she began to whimper, desperate, "No, Madame Favart, you must keep Picasso, you get better. If you sell Picasso, I take you to Japan, new treatment."

Phew, she believes me, thought Aimée, and she immediately cried out, "It's for you, Kumiko, for you, I insist. Come on, let's not waste time, I've only got a few days left. Here, I've prepared the documents. Go quick and get some witnesses out in the corridor, that way I can leave with an easy conscience."

Aimée signed the necessary documents in the presence of the doctor and the nurse; they added their initials. Shaking with tears, Kumiko gathered up the papers and promised to come back the next day as early as possible. She took an unbearably long time to leave, and kept blowing kisses to Aimée until she had disappeared at the end of the corridor.

Relieved, alone at last, Aimée smiled to the ceiling.

Poor goose, she thought, go on and dream about your wealth: you will be even more disappointed once I'm dead. And then you'll really have a good reason to cry. Between now and then I hope I never see you again.

No doubt that God in whom Aimée did not believe actually heard her, because at dawn she fell into a coma and, a few days later, although she never realized it, a dose of morphine ended her life.

Forty years later, Kumiko Kruk, the wealthiest person in Japan, global queen of the cosmetics industry, now an ambassador for Unicef, an old woman adored by the media for her success, her charisma, and her generosity, stood before the press and justified her humanitarian actions:

"If I invest part of my profit in the fight against hunger, and to make medical care available to the poorest populations, it is in memory of a dear French friend from my youth, Aimée Favart, who on her deathbed offered me a painting by Picasso that enabled me, when I sold it, to found my company. Although I was practically a stranger to her, she insisted on giving me this priceless gift. Ever since that time, it has seemed logical to me that my profits should, in turn, go to help other strangers. That woman, Aimée Favart, was all love. She believed in humanity like no one else. She passed her values on to me, and that, more than any precious Picasso, is without a doubt her greatest gift."

EVERY REASON
TO BE HAPPY

To be honest, nothing would have happened if I hadn't changed my hairdresser.

My life would have gone on as peacefully as before, with every outward sign of happiness, had I not been so impressed by Stacy's extraordinary look when she got back from vacation. Completely renewed! She'd been a middle-aged middle-class frump, worn down by four kids, and now her short cut had transformed her into a pretty, sporty, go-get-'em blonde. At the time I suspected her of having cut her hair in order to distract attention from some successful cosmetic surgery—that's what all my friends do when they've had a facelift—but, once I'd satisfied myself that her face had not undergone any sort of surgical act, I acknowledged that she had found the ideal hairstylist.

"Ideal, darling, absolutely ideal. The Atelier Capillaire on the rue Victor Hugo. I'd already heard about it a while ago but you know how it is, same thing with our hairdressers as with our husbands: we can go for years thinking we've got the best one around!"

I refrained from making any sarcastic remarks about the vanity of the name of the place—"Capillary Studio," indeed—but just wrote down that I had to ask for David and tell him Stacy sent me—"He's a genius, darling, an absolute genius."

That very evening, I warned Samuel about my upcoming metamorphosis.

"I think I'm going to change my hairstylist."

He looked at me with surprise for a few seconds.

"What for? You're fine as you are."

"Oh, yes, I know you're always pleased with me like this, you never criticize me."

"You can fault me with being an unquestioning admirer . . . But what is it you don't like about your look?"

"Nothing in particular. I just need a change."

He took careful note of my declaration as if beyond its frivolity lay some deeper consideration; and his watchful stare drove me to change the topic of conversation and then to leave the room, because I had no desire to offer myself up as subject matter for his perspicacity. While my husband's redeeming feature may be his extreme attentiveness toward my person, at times this weighs upon me: my most insignificant words are parsed, analyzed, decrypted to such a degree that to make light of it I often tell my girlfriends that I feel like I've married my psychoanalyst.

"Don't complain!" they all say. "You've got money, he's good-looking, he's intelligent, he loves you, and he listens to everything you say! What more do you want? Children?"

"No, not yet."

"Then you've got every reason to be happy."

Every reason to be happy. Are there any other platitudes I hear more often than this one? Do people say this just as often when referring to others, or do they just use it for my sake? The moment I start expressing myself with even a hint of freedom, I get the phrase tossed into my face: "You have every reason to be happy." It's as if people were shouting at me—"Shut up, you have no right to complain"—then slamming the door in my face. And yet I have no intention of complaining, I'm just trying to give accurate—and humorous—expression to slight feelings of discomfort. Maybe it's something to do with the tone of my voice, similar to my mother's, a little damp and whiny, that gives people the impression I'm complaining? Or could it be that my status as a rich well-married heiress precludes me from sharing any sort of complex thoughts in public? Once or twice I was afraid that in spite of myself I might let my secret transpire through my words. But this fear hardly lasted longer than a shiver, for I am sure that I can control myself to perfection. With the exception of Samuel and myself—and a few specialists, silenced by professional discretion—not a soul knows of my secret.

Thus, I went to the Atelier Capillaire on the rue Victor Hugo and, honestly, I had to keep focused on the miracle they'd performed on Stacy in order to put up with the reception they inflicted upon me. Priestesses draped in white robes bombarded me with questions about my health, my eating habits, the sports I practiced, and the history of my hair, in order to establish my "capillary appraisal." After that, they left me for ten minutes on some Indian cushions with an herbal tea that smelled of cow manure, then finally they introduced me to David, who announced triumphantly that he would be taking care of me, as if he were inducting me into a sect now that I'd successfully passed some exam. The worst of it was that I felt obliged to thank him.

We went upstairs, where a superb salon with pure, simple lines had been arranged in a style that said, "Watch out, I've been inspired by the millennial wisdom of India." At that point an army of barefooted vestal virgins offered to take care of me: manicure, pedicure, massage.

David studied me carefully, while I observed the way his shirt opened onto his hairy chest, and I wondered if this were a requirement in order to become a hairdresser. Then he declared: "I'm going to shorten your hair, make the color slightly darker at the roots, then flatten it against your scalp on the right hand side and enhance the volume on the left. Totally asymmetrical. You need something like this. Otherwise your face, which is very regular, will end up in prison. We need to liberate your fantasy. We need air, quickly, air! Something unexpected."

I smiled in response, but if I'd had the courage to be honest, I'd have got up and left right then and there. I hate people who have perfect aim, anyone who gets anywhere near my secret, to the point where they might come close to detecting it. But this time I reasoned that it would be better to overlook such comments, and make the most of this Figaro so that he'd give me the sort of look that would help me conceal my secret all the better.

"What an adventure," I exclaimed, to encourage him.

"Would you like us to do your hands at the same time?"

"Yes, that would be nice."

And that is when fate played its hand. He called out to a certain Nathalie, who was putting beauty products away on the shelves. No sooner did Nathalie lay eyes on me than she dropped the jars she had in her hands.

The crash of shattering glass destroyed the pervasive serenity of the scalp sanctuary. Nathalie blurted an apology and fell to her knees to begin sweeping up the mess.

"I didn't know I had such an effect on her," joked David, to make light of the incident.

I nodded, although there was no fooling me: I had been all too aware of how Nathalie panicked, as if it were a blast of wind on my cheek. It was the sight of me that had frightened her. Why? I didn't get the impression that I knew her—I'm a fairly good physiognomist—but I cast about in my memories all the same.

When she was back on her feet David said, in a gentle voice tense with irritation: "Right, Nathalie, Madame and I are waiting for you."

She went pale, and wrung her hands.

"I . . . I don't feel well, David."

David left my side for a few minutes and went into the

changingroom with her. A few seconds later he came back, followed by another employee.

"Shakira will take care of you."

"Is Nathalie ill?"

"Women's trouble, I imagine," he said, with a scorn addressed to all women and their incomprehensible moods.

When he realized he had allowed a whiff of his misogyny to escape, he took hold of himself and subsequently filled his conversation with charm.

When I left the Atelier Capillaire, I had to admit that Stacy had been right: David was an absolute genius with color and scissors. I lingered next to every shop window where I could see my reflection, and gazed at a lovely, smiling stranger, whom I found very pleasing.

It took Samuel's breath away when he saw me walk into the living room—well, I had delayed my entry somewhat to make sure I was ready. Not only did he compliment me, never taking his eyes off me, but he also insisted on taking me to the Maison Blanche, my favorite restaurant, so that everyone could see what a lovely woman he'd married.

All this effusion of joy eclipsed the incident with the manicure and the panicked young woman. But I figured I didn't have to wait until I really needed a new cut to go back to the Atelier Capillaire, so I decided to try some of the other treatments on offer: and the same thing happened.

Three times over, Nathalie went to pieces on seeing me, and found ways not to come anywhere near me, to avoid greeting or serving me, and to hide herself away in the back rooms.

Her attitude was so astonishing that I was intrigued. The woman must have been in her forties, like me; she was lithe in her movements, with a narrow waist and fairly large hips, thin arms, and long, powerful hands. With her head tilted to one side, she would go down on her knees to lavish her care on her clients, a picture of humility. Although she was working in a trendy, elegant sanctum, unlike her colleagues she did not take herself for a minister of luxury; on the contrary, she carried herself like a devoted servant, silent, almost slave-like . . . If she had not fled from me, I should even have found her to be very convivial company . . . After racking my brain into the remotest corners, I came away convinced that she and I had never met, nor could I suspect I might have been at the origin of some sort of professional setback where she was concerned, for while I am president of the Foundation of Contemporary Visual Arts, I am not involved with hiring and firing.

After a few sessions, I was able to pinpoint her fear: she was afraid, more than anything, that I might notice her. She did not seem to feel either spite or animosity toward me; she simply wanted to become transparent the moment I appeared. Consequently, I saw no one else.

I came to the conclusion that she must be harboring a secret. As an expert in dissimulation, I could trust my own judgment.

And this is how I came to commit the irreparable: I followed her.

I sat myself down behind the curtain of the brasserie adjacent to the Atelier Capillaire, with a hat on my head and my face hidden by huge dark glasses, and I kept a look-out as the employees left the building. Just as I expected, Nathalie waved a hasty goodbye to her coworkers, and went alone down into the metro.

I rushed down after her, pleased that I had thought to anticipate by buying a supply of tickets.

I was so discreet that she did not notice me either in the carriage or when changing trains; the rush hour helped, too. Jolted back and forth by the movement of the train, shoved here and there by the other passengers, I found the situation absurd and entertaining. I had never followed a man, let alone a woman, and my heart was beating fit to burst, just like when I was a child trying out a new game.

She got out at Place d'Italie and went into a shopping center. I feared several times that I might bump into her because she was clearly a regular there. She was very quick at buying what she needed for dinner and, unlike in the public transportation, she moved about boldly and comfortably in her surroundings.

Finally, with her shopping bags in hand, she set off down the little streets in Butte-aux-Cailles, a working-class neighborhood consisting of modest little houses—revolutionary, once upon a time; a century ago, poor workers crowded into these small houses, neglected, far from the center, at the very edge of the capital; nowadays, the recently wealthy bought up all the property to pay for the impression—given the sum involved—of owning a *hôtel particulier* right in the heart of Paris. Could a simple employee possibly live here?

She reassured me by going beyond the leafy, residential streets and on into the zone that had remained working-class. Warehouses, factories, vacant lots cluttered with scrap metal. She went through a huge gate of weather-beaten boards, crossed the courtyard, and vanished into a tiny gray house with worn shutters.

There. I was at the end of my investigation. I may have had fun, but I hadn't learned a thing. What else could I try? I studied the names on the buzzers of the courtyard's inhabitants and the warehouses. Nothing meant a thing to me; in passing, I did recognize the name of a famous stuntman, and I recalled seeing a program that showed how he prepared his stunts, in this very courtyard.

And so?

I was no further forward. Although I'd had fun trailing her, it hadn't taught me anything. I still didn't know why this woman panicked whenever she saw me.

I was about to go back the way I'd come, when I saw something that forced me to lean against the wall not to fall over. How was this possible? Could I be going mad?

I closed my eyes and then opened them again, as if I could wipe away the trick my imagination was playing upon my brain. I leaned forward. For the second time I looked at the figure heading down the street.

Yes. It was him. I had just seen Samuel.

Samuel, my husband, but twenty years younger . . .

The young man was striding nonchalantly down the hill. On his back he had a schoolbag, full of books, that weighed no more than a sports bag. In his ears a walkman throbbed with a music that gave a supple swing to his step.

He went past me, gave me a polite smile, crossed the yard and went into Nathalie's house.

It took me a few minutes before I was able to move. My brain had immediately grasped the situation, while the major part of me resisted it, refused it. When the young man walked by me, with his smooth, white skin, his thick hair, and his long legs with their loutish, rolling gait, the desire I felt for him was extremely powerful, as if I were abruptly falling in love; and this did not help me accept the truth of what was going on. I wanted to grab his face in my hands and devour his lips. What was happening to me? Ordinarily I was not so . . . Ordinarily, I was just the opposite . . .

This chance encounter with my husband's son—his exact double, only twenty years younger—filled me with amorous exaltation. I should have been jealous of this woman above anything else, but instead I wanted to throw myself into her son's arms.

It seemed like I really was not doing anything normally.

No doubt that is why this story had to happen in the first place . . .

It took me hours to find my way back. In fact, I must have been stumbling my way along, unaware of anything, until night fell and a taxi rank reminded me that I had to go home. Fortunately Samuel was busy with a conference that evening: I did not have to give him any explanations, nor was I able to ask him for any.

In the days that followed, to hide my devastation, I pretended I had a migraine; Samuel was very worried. I looked on him with new eyes as he took care of me: did he know that I knew? Surely not. If he had a double life, how did he manage to show such devotion?

Concerned about my condition, he lightened his workload so that he could take the time to come home and have lunch with me every day. Anyone who had not seen what I had seen would never have suspected my husband. He behaved perfectly. If he were play-acting, he was the greatest actor in the world. His tenderness seemed genuine: his perspiring anxiety could not be faked, nor could he mime the relief he felt whenever I could invent some improvement for myself.

I began to have doubts. Not that I had seen his son, but that Samuel could still be seeing this woman. Did he even know? Did he know she had given him a son? Perhaps it was just some old affair, a little fling from before; perhaps this Nathalie, disappointed to hear about his marriage to me, had hidden her pregnancy, and kept the boy for herself. How old was he? Eighteen . . . So it would have been just before he and I fell in love . . . I managed to convince myself that that must be what had happened. She'd been abandoned, so she had a child behind his back. That was clearly the reason for her fear whenever she saw me: she was filled with remorse. Besides, she did not look at all like a bad woman, but rather like one who has been eroded by melancholy.

After a week of so-called migraines, I decided that I felt better. I delivered Samuel, and myself, from our worries, and begged him to make up for his lost time at work; in exchange, he made me swear to call him if I had the slightest concern.

I stayed hardly more than an hour at the Foundation, just long enough to make sure that everything was running smoothly without me. Without telling anyone, I went deep into the bowels of Paris and took the metro for the Place d'Italie, as if there were no other way to reach that strange and threatening place other than subterraneously.

I had no real plan, no pre-established strategy, but I had to corroborate my hypothesis. It was fairly easy to find the cheerless street where the boy lived with his mother, and I sat on the first bench I found that would allow me to keep an eye on the gate.

What did I hope to do? Go up to neighbors. Chat with the residents. Find something out, one way or another.

After two hours of waiting in vain, I felt like a cigarette. Strange for a woman who does not smoke? Yes. It amused me. In fact, for a while now I had been acting in a very unusual way—trailing strangers, taking public transportation, discovering my husband's past, waiting on a bench, buying cigarettes. I set off, therefore, to look for a *bureau de tabac.*

What brand should I buy? I had no experience of cigarettes.

"I'll have the same," I said to the tobacconist, who had just served a neighborhood regular.

He handed me a pack, and waited for me to give him the exact change like any good addict familiar with the price of her pleasure. I gave him a note that I hoped would suffice, in exchange for which he gave me a grumble and more notes and a lot of coins.

As I turned around, there he was.

Samuel.

Well, Samuel the younger. Samuel's son.

He laughed when he saw my surprise.

"Excuse me, I startled you."

"No, I'm the clumsy one, I failed to notice there was anyone behind me."

He moved aside to let me by, and bought some mints. As pleasant and well brought up as his father, I could not help but think. I felt an immense liking for him; even more than that, something inexpressible . . . As if, intoxicated with his smell, his animal proximity, I could not resolve myself to see him walk away.

I ran out after him into the street and called out, "Sir, excuse me . . ."

Taken aback at being called Sir by a woman older than himself—how old must he have thought I was?—he looked around quickly to make sure I was really talking to him, then waited for me on the opposite sidewalk.

I quickly dreamt up a lie.

"Excuse me for disturbing you, I'm a journalist and I'm doing a story on today's young people. Would it be taking up too much of your time to ask you a few questions?"

"What—you mean now, here?"

"Well, we could go for a drink, in the café where you frightened me."

He smiled, intrigued by the idea.

"Which newspaper?"

"*Le Monde.*"

An approving flick of his eyelashes showed that he was flattered to collaborate with such a prestigious newspaper.

"I'd be glad to. But I don't know if I'm really representative of today's young people. Sometimes I really feel out of synch."

"I don't want you to be representative of modern youth, I want you to be representative of yourself."

My phrase convinced him, and he followed me.

We ordered two coffees, and began to talk.

"Aren't you going to take notes?"

"I'll start taking them when I've lost my memory."

He sent me a glance full of praise, never for a moment suspecting that everything that came out of my mouth thereafter was pure bluffing.

"How old are you?"

"Fifteen."

Right off the bat, my main hypothesis was shattered to pieces. Fifteen years ago, Samuel and I had been married for two years . . .

I used the pretext that I needed more sugar to move, get up, walk around for a few seconds and sit back down.

"What are you hoping for in life?"

"I love the cinema. I'd like to become a filmmaker."

"Who are your favorite directors?"

Now that he was off on a subject he was passionate about, the young man could have talked forever, and this gave me time to think about my next question.

"Is this passion for the cinema something that comes from your family?"

He burst out laughing.

"I really doubt it!"

He suddenly seemed to be proud of having acquired rather than inherited his tastes.

"What about your mother?"

"My mother is more the TV series type, you know, that crap that lasts for weeks with family secrets and illegitimate kids and crimes of passion and so on and so forth . . ."

"What does she do for a living?"

"Odd jobs. For a long time she worked taking care of old people in their homes. Now she's working at a beauty salon."

"And your father?"

He grew reticent.

"Is all this part of your story?"

"I don't want to force you to have to say anything indiscreet. Rest assured that I'll use a false name for you and I won't say anything that might make it possible to recognize either you or your parents."

"Oh, okay, great."

"What I'm looking for is how you relate with the adult world—the way you see things, the way you position your future in that world. That's why your relationship with your father is significant. Unless he has died; if so, please forgive me."

It had suddenly occurred to me that Nathalie might have made him believe that Samuel had died in order to justify his absence. I trembled at the thought I might have hurt this poor boy.

"No, he's not dead."

"Oh . . . absent, then?"

He hesitated. I was suffering as much as he was from this dilemma.

"What's his name?"

"Samuel."

I was crushed. I no longer knew how to go on, how to keep playing my role. I alleged a new desire for sugar, went to the counter and came back. Quick, quick now! Come up with something!

When I sat back down, he was the one who had changed. He was relaxed, and the smile on his face showed his willingness to open up.

"Well, I suppose because you're going to use false names, I can tell you everything."

"Of course," I said, trying to keep from trembling.

He settled himself more comfortably on his chair.

"My father is an amazing guy. He doesn't live with us, even though he's been crazy in love with my mother for sixteen years."

"Why not?"

"Because he's married."

"Does he have other children?"

"No."

"So why doesn't he leave his wife?"

"Because she's crazy."

"I beg your pardon?"

"She's completely out to lunch. She'd kill him, on the spot. Or worse. She's capable of anything. I think at the same time he feels sorry for her. So to make up for it he's really kind to us—Mom and my sisters and me—and he's convinced us that this is the best way."

"Oh? You have sisters?"

"Yes, two little sisters, ten and twelve."

Although the boy went on talking, I could no longer hear a thing: my head was whirling. I could make no sense of what he was telling me—even though it should have been of capital interest—because I kept coming up against what I had just learned: Samuel had a second home, an entire family, and he stayed with me on the pretext that I was unhinged.

How convincing was my sudden leave-taking? I have no idea. In any event, I called for a taxi, and the moment I was hidden behind the car windows I burst into tears.

The weeks that followed were the worst in my life.

I had lost my bearings.

Samuel seemed like a total stranger to me. Everything I thought I knew about him, all my respect for him, the trust on which my love had been founded: it had all vanished. He was leading a double life, he loved another woman in another part of Paris, a woman he'd had three children with.

It was the existence of the children, more than anything, that tormented me. Because there I was in no position to fight back. A woman was someone I could compete with, although there would always be certain issues . . . but children . . .

I wept for entire days and could not hide my tears from Samuel. After trying to talk with me, he begged me to go back to my psychiatrist.

"My psychiatrist? Why *my* psychiatrist?"

"Because you've been there before."

"Why are you insinuating, that he's mine? Was he invented to provide care for me and me alone?"

"Sorry. I said 'your psychiatrist' when I should have said 'our psychiatrist,' since we went to him for years."

"Yes! For all the good it did."

"It was very useful, Isabelle, it helped us to accept ourselves as we are, and to live with our fate. I'll make an appointment for you."

"Why do you want me to see a psychiatrist, I'm not crazy," I screamed.

"No, you're not crazy. But when you have a toothache, you go to the dentist's, and when you have something hurting in your soul, you go to the psychiatrist. You're just going to have to trust me on this, I can't leave you in this state."

"Why? You're going to leave me, is that it?"

"What are you going on about? I am saying, on the contrary, that I can't leave you like this!"

"'Leave me.' You said 'leave me?'"

"You're really at the end of your rope, Isabelle. And I get the feeling that I'm upsetting you when I should be making you calmer."

"Well, at least you're right on that score!"

"Have I done something wrong? Tell me. Tell me so we can get it over with."

"'Get it over with!' You see, you want to leave me."

He took me in his arms, and despite my gestures of protest, he managed to hold me tenderly against him.

"I love you, you hear me? And I don't want to leave you. If I had wanted to, I would have done it a long time ago. When . . ."

"I know. No point bringing that up."

"It would do us good to talk about it from time to time."

"No. Useless. Taboo. We won't go there. No one can get through. Finished."

He sighed.

Lying against his chest, his shoulders, lulled by the warm tone of his voice, I managed to calm down. The moment he gave me the slip, I would start brooding again. Was Samuel staying with me for my money? Anyone who saw our situation from the outside would say so, because he was no more than an editorial consultant for a major publishing group, and I had inherited millions in investments and real estate; I was well acquainted with Samuel's scrupulous attitude toward my capital: the reason he had continued working after we got married was so that he would not be dependent on me, and so that he could offer me gifts with his "own money"; he had refused all my attempts to set up a trust for him, and had insisted on our drawing up a marriage contract that excluded communal property. The total opposite of an interested, avid spouse. Why did he stay with me if he had a wife and children elsewhere? Perhaps he didn't love that woman enough to share a life with her? Yes, that could be it . . . He didn't dare to tell her . . . She looked so ordinary . . . he used me as a pretext so that he wouldn't have to get stuck with a manicurist . . . Basically, he preferred my company . . . But his children? I knew Samuel: how could he resist the desire to live with his children, to do his duty by them? Something very powerful must be motivating him, enough to keep him from them . . . What could it be? Me? When I couldn't give him children? Or was it cowardice? A fundamental cowardice? That cowardice my friends consider to be men's principal characteristic . . . At the end of the afternoon, as I could not settle on any one idea, I eventually concluded that his young son was right: I must have slid into madness.

My condition got worse. As did Samuel's. Through some sort of strange empathy, dark circles weighed down his exhausted eyes, apprehension tightened his features, and I could hear how he huffed and puffed as he climbed the stairs of our *hôtel particulier* to join me in the room I no longer left.

He asked me to be frank, to explain the source of my pain. Naturally, that would have been the best course, and yet I refused. Since childhood I have had a sort of counterproductive talent: I invariably avoid the right solution. No doubt if I had spoken to him or asked him to speak, we might have avoided the catastrophe . . .

Stubborn, hard, wounded, I said nothing, and I stared at him as an enemy would. No matter how I thought of him, he could only come across as a traitor: if it was not me that he was deceiving, then it was his mistress and her children. Did he care for too many things, or did he care for nothing? Was this man before me someone who could not make up his mind, or the most cynical man on the planet? Who was he?

I wore myself out with suspicion. I had lost my way, I could not even remember to eat and drink, and grew so weak that eventually they had to inject me with vitamins and hydrate me with a drip.

Samuel did not look all that robust himself. And he refused to look after himself, since I was the one who was suffering. I enjoyed watching him worry, much as an old mistress gnaws on the last bone of love; it would never have occurred to me to go beyond my own selfishness and demand that he be looked after, too.

It was surely Samuel who sent for Dr. Feldenheim, my former psychiatrist.

Although I would have greatly liked to reveal my thoughts to him, for three sessions I resisted.

By the fourth one, tired of beating around the bush, I told him what I had discovered: the mistress, the children, the clandestine home.

"So that is it," he concluded. "It was time you spat it out."

"Oh really? Is that what you think? It seems to fuel your curiosity, Doctor. For me, it doesn't change a thing."

"My dear Isabelle, at the risk of surprising you and above all of being excluded from my profession, I am going to break my vow of confidentiality: I have been aware of the situation for several years."

"Pardon?"

"Since Florian was born."

"Florian? Who is Florian?"

"The young man you interrogated, Samuel's son."

To hear him speaking in such a familiar way about the very people who were destroying my relationship and my happiness . . . I could feel the anger welling up inside me.

"Is it Samuel who told you this?"

"Yes. When his son was born. I believe it was a secret he found too heavy to keep."

"What a monster!"

"Don't be too hasty, Isabelle. Have you stopped to consider how difficult this situation is for Samuel?"

"Are you joking? He has every reason to be happy."

"Isabelle, don't try that with me. Don't forget that I know. I am well aware of the fact that you have a rare disease—"

"Be quiet."

"No. Not talking about it creates more problems than solutions."

"And anyway, no one knows what it is."

"Female impotence? Samuel knows. He married a beautiful, funny, sexy woman, whom he adores, and he has never been able to make love to her. He has never penetrated her. Has never shared an orgasm with her. Your body is closed off to him, Isabelle, despite the numerous attempts, despite all the therapy. Can you imagine the frustration he must feel from time to time?"

"From time to time? All the time, would you believe. All

the time! And yet, no matter how I hate myself, no matter how guilty I feel, it doesn't change a thing. There are times I think it would have been better if he'd abandoned me when we found out, seventeen years ago!"

"And yet, he stayed. Do you know why?"

"Yes. For my money!"

"Isabelle, don't try that with me."

"Because I'm out of my mind!"

"Isabelle, please: don't try that with me. Why, then?"

"Out of pity."

"No. Because he loves you."

A thick inner silence came over me. I had just been buried beneath a layer of snow.

"Yes, he loves you. Samuel may still be a man like any other, a normal man who needs to penetrate a woman's flesh and have children, but he loves you and continues to love you. He could not bring himself to leave you. Besides, he doesn't want to. Your marriage has taught him to behave like a saint. This justifies his desire to have other experiences outside your marriage. One day he met this woman, Nathalie; he thought that by having a relationship with her, and then a child, he would have the desire, the strength, to leave you. In vain. He found that he had to subject his new family to distance and absence. No doubt the children don't know the truth but Nathalie does, and she's accepted it. So you see, nothing has been simple for Samuel these sixteen years. He wears himself out at work trying to make enough money for his two families, to bring you presents and to give them enough to live on; he's exhausted from making himself available and attentive to both sides; he hardly looks after himself, only you, and the others. Add to that the fact that he is riddled with guilt. For not living with Nathalie, and his son, and his daughters, he feels guilty; and for lying to you for such a long time, he feels guilty too."

"Well then, just let him make up his mind! Decide one way

or the other! Let him go to them! I'm not the one who would stop him."

"Isabelle, he can never do that."

"And why not?"

"He loves you."

"Samuel?"

"It tears him apart, it's a passion, it's incomprehensible and indestructible, but he does loves you."

"Samuel . . ."

"More than anything."

With these words, Dr. Feldenheim stood up and left the room.

Filled with a newfound sweetness, I no longer struggled against myself or against this Samuel who was a stranger to me. He loved me. He loved me so much that he had hidden his double life from me, and had imposed it upon a woman who was capable of offering her body to him and giving him children. Samuel . . .

In raptures, I waited for him. I was eager to take his face between my palms, to place a kiss on his forehead and thank him for his unfailing love. I was going to declare my own to him, my own ugly love, capable of doubt, and furor, and jealousy, my horrible, filthy love, that had only just, quite abruptly, become pure. He would find out that I understood him, that he must hide nothing from me, that I wanted to allocate part of my fortune to his family. If they were his family, then they were mine as well. I was going to show him that I could rise above bourgeois propriety. Just as he did. Out of love.

At seven o'clock, Stacy stopped by to find out how I was doing. She was reassured to find me smiling and calm.

"I'm so happy to see you like this, after all those weeks of sobbing. You are completely changed."

"And it's not the Atelier Capillaire," I said with a laugh, "it's because I've realized I married a wonderful man."

"Samuel? What woman would not want such a man?"

"I'm lucky, aren't I?"

"You? It's downright indecent. There are times when I find it hard to remain your friend—you have every reason to be happy."

Stacy left at eight o'clock. Determined to put an end to my apathy, I went down to the pantry to help the cook make some dinner.

At nine o'clock, although Samuel had not yet come back, I decided not to worry.

At ten o'clock, I was at the end of my tether. I had already left twenty messages on his cell phone, which recorded my words without replying.

At eleven o'clock I was so tense with anxiety that I got dressed, got into the car, and without giving it any further thought, set off for the Place d'Italie.

When I got to the Butte-aux-Cailles, I found the gate wide open and people coming and going outside the little gray house.

I rushed forward, went through the open door, down the hall, headed toward the light and found Nathalie collapsed in an armchair, surrounded by her children and the neighbors.

"Where is Samuel?" I asked.

Nathalie raised her eyes, and recognized me. A trace of panic flickered across her dark eyes.

"Please, tell me," I repeated, "where is Samuel?"

"He's dead. Just now. At six o'clock. A heart attack, while he was playing tennis with Florian."

Why do I never have a normal reaction to things? Instead of going to pieces, or sobbing, or screaming, I turned to Florian, who was crying, and I pulled him to his feet, and held him close, to console him.

THE BAREFOOT
PRINCESS

He was very impatient to see her again.

While the bus carrying the little troupe began to climb the road winding up to the Sicilian village, he could think of nothing else. Perhaps he'd signed on to this tour for no other reason than to come back here? Otherwise, why would he have accepted? He didn't like the play very much, his role even less, and for all his troubles he would only be receiving a pittance. To be sure, he no longer really had the choice: either he must accept this sort of engagement, or give up his acting career forever and get what his family would call "a real job." It had been years since he had had the leisure to choose his roles; his time of glory had lasted for only one or two seasons at the very start of his career, when he had irresistible good looks and no one had realized yet how deplorable his acting was.

And it was then that he'd met her, the mysterious woman, in this town set like a crown on a rocky mountain. Had she changed? Surely. But not so very much.

And he had not changed all that much himself. Fabio had preserved his leading man's physique, although he no longer had either the youth or the brilliance of a typical lead actor. No, if he no longer got the good roles these days it was not because his looks had gone downhill—he was still just as attractive to women—but because his talent was not on a par with his appearance. It didn't bother him to talk about it, even with his colleagues or with directors, because he considered that looks and talent were both innate gifts. He had received one of them, and was lacking the other. And where was the harm in that? Not everyone could have a career at the top; he was content with his minor career, it was enough for him. For what he liked was not the acting itself—if that had been the case, he could have tried to improve—but the lifestyle that went with it. Traveling, camaraderie, playfulness, applause, restaurants, girls for a night. Yes, he'd rather have that life any day than the one ordained him. With Fabio you could be sure of one thing: he would do everything in his power for as long as possible to avoid returning to his place on the family farm.

"A peasant's son, handsome as a prince": so went the title, in his early years, of a television commentary devoted to him when he was starring in a series that had held all of Italy in thrall over the space of a summer. *The Prince Leocadio.* His starring role. It had earned him thousands of letters from his female admirers, some provocative, others flattering, others intriguing; all of them in love. *Prince Leocadio* had led to a role in a Franco-Germano-Italian series about a flamboyant multimillionaire. That was the role that had reduced him to poverty. Not only had the initial novelty of his looks worn off, but the character—excessive, ambiguous, full of contradictions—called for a real actor. The moment the filming began he was dubbed "the male model," a nickname which was taken up by the press when commenting on his pathetic performance. Subsequently, Fabio appeared on screen on only two more occasions, once in Germany, and once in France—because in those countries, his flamboyant multimillionaire role had been dubbed by real professionals, thus creating the illusion that he was a better actor than in reality. After that, nothing. Nothing of note. That winter, seeing reruns of *Prince Leocadio* at four in the morning, he had rediscovered himself with some dismay: he hated the inept plot, his inconsistent partners (who had vanished like him), and above all the tight costumes, the ridiculous shoes with heels, the voluminous hair style that made him look like some actress in a second-rate American sitcom, with that lock of hair dangling over his right eye, depriving him of his gaze and making his regular features seem even more unexpressive. In short, the only excuse, the sole justification for his performance onscreen, was the fact that he was only twenty years old.

As the bus rounded the bend, the medieval citadel appeared: proud, sovereign, its tall ramparts and half-moon towers commanding respect. Did she still live there? How would he find her—he did not even know her name. "Call me Donatella," she had murmured. At the time he had believed that to be her name; several years later, when he would think back over her words, he became certain that she had given him a pseudonym.

Why had that adventure had such an impact upon him? Why, fifteen years later, was he still thinking about it, even though he had known dozens of women in the interim?

No doubt because Donatella had been so mysterious at the time, and remained so. Women are pleasing because they come to us wrapped in the catkin of an enigma, and they cease to please when they lose their intrigue. Do women believe that men are only interested in what is between their legs? That would be an error: men are more attracted by a woman's romantic side than by her sexuality. And if proof were needed: if men stray, blame it on the days, not the nights. Days spent talking in harsh sunlight do more to tarnish a woman's aura than the nights spent in each other's arms. Fabio often felt like declaring to women: preserve the nights and remove the days, you will hold on to your man longer. Yet he kept his thoughts to himself, out of caution to a certain degree, for fear of driving them away; but to a larger degree because he was convinced they would not understand: they would merely see it as confirmation that men only thought about fucking, whereas what he meant to imply was that the greatest playboys—like himself—are actually mystics in search of mystery, and they will always prefer that part of the female creature that is not given to the one that is readily abandoned.

Donatella appeared before him on an evening in May, backstage at the local theater after the performance. This was two years after his triumphant beginnings on television, and he had already begun his descent. At that point they no longer sought his screen presence, but because he was slightly famous, he had been offered a major role on stage: he would perform *Le Cid* by Corneille, a veritable marathon of verse tirades, which he scrupulously recited without understanding a word. What made him happy when he left the stage was not that he had acted well but that he'd made it to the end without any mistakes, like some athlete going an unusual distance. At the time he was not as lucid as he was today, yet he did sense that the audience appreciated his face above all, or perhaps his legs, enhanced by the tights he wore.

A huge wicker basket full of yellow and brown orchids had been left outside his dressing room before the show. There was no card with the basket. During the performance, when he was not called on to recite, Fabio could not help but look out into the audience to try to guess who might have sent him the sumptuous gift. But the spotlights blinded him and prevented him from any closer scrutiny of the faces protected by the half-light; and then, of course, he had the wretched play to perform . . .

After a worthy amount of applause, Fabio hurried to his dressing room, took a quick shower, and splashed himself with cologne, because he had the suspicion that the person behind the gift might show up.

Donatella was waiting for him in the corridor backstage.

Fabio saw a very young woman, her long hair restrained on either side in a braided crown; she gave him a graceful handshake.

Steeped in the chivalry that went with his role, Fabio spontaneously kissed the lady's hand, something he rarely did.

"Was it you?" he asked, referring to the orchids.

"It was I," she nodded, lowering heavy eyelids with brilliant black lashes.

Her limbs seemed to emerge furtively from a flowing dress in silk or chiffon—he did not know which—something light, airy, costly, oriental, something a woman with a supple, soft body would choose, a woman who hardly weighs a thing. Around her white wrist she wore a slave bracelet, although the expression "slave bracelet" was far from appropriate where she was concerned: it was as if you were admiring a woman who orders her slaves about, or even transforms other human beings into slaves, a sort of Cleopatra, yes, a Cleopatra reigning from a mountain in Sicily, so great was the imperious strength she conveyed, a mixture of sensuality, shyness, and something altogether wild.

"I am inviting you to dinner. Would you like that?"

Was there any point in answering her question? Did he even give her an answer?

Fabio remembered that he had given her his arm, and they left together.

Once they were outside in the cobbled streets of the historic village, beneath a veiled moon, he saw that she was barefoot. She noticed his surprise and anticipated his question: "Yes, I feel more free, like this."

Her words, her manner were so natural that no response was possible.

It was a magnificent walk, on an evening where perfumes of jasmine, fennel, and anise arose from between the cool city walls. Arm in arm they climbed silently toward the highest part of the citadel. There they came upon a five-star inn, the most luxurious place imaginable.

As she was heading for the entrance, he reached out to hold

her back: under no circumstances could he afford to take a conquest there.

Donatella must have read his thoughts, for she reassured him: "Don't worry. They have been notified. They are expecting us."

When they entered the lobby, all the staff members were indeed lined up on either side of the entrance and bowed down to them. As Fabio led the ravishing young woman past the impeccable staff, it was as if he were guiding a bride to the altar.

Although they were the only patrons in the fine restaurant, they were seated in a private dining room, in order to enjoy a certain intimacy.

The maître d' addressed the young woman with excessive courtesy, calling her "Princess." The wine waiter did the same. As did the chef. Fabio concluded that she must belong to the nobility, staying here as she did, and that it was no doubt out of respect for her rank that they overlooked her eccentricities and did not mind if she came to dinner in her bare feet.

They were served caviar and superb wines; one dish followed the other, all inventive, delicious, exceptional. The conversation between the two diners remained poetic: they talked about the play, the theater, the cinema, love, feelings. Fabio quickly understood that he must avoid asking personal questions of the princess because she withdrew at the slightest inquiry. He also discovered that she had wished to dine with him because she had delighted in the two series that had made him famous; to his utmost surprise, even as he was greatly impressed by her person, he realized that, with the unexpected help of the two romantic heroes he had incarnated, he made just as great an impression on her.

During dessert he took the liberty of holding her hand; she let him move closer; he told her with a newfound delicacy, worthy of his characters, that he dreamt of only one thing, to be able to take her in his arms; she trembled, lowered her eyelids, trembled again then murmured breathlessly, "Come with me."

They headed toward the grand staircase leading up to the rooms, and she escorted Fabio to her suite, the most luxurious chambers he had ever seen, an exuberance of velvet and silk, enhanced with embroidery, Persian rugs, ivory trays, marquetry seats, crystal carafes, and silver goblets.

She closed the door behind her and, untying the wispy scarf she had around her neck, conveyed beyond a doubt that she was offering herself to him.

Was it because of the décor, worthy of an oriental tale? Was it because of the voluptuous food and drink? Was it because of the girl herself—so strange, rebellious and restrained, sophisticated and savage, all at the same time? Whatever the reason, Fabio's night of love was exceptional, the most beautiful he had ever known. And it was something that today, fifteen years later, he was more sure of than ever.

That long-ago morning, at first light, he emerged from his lover's sleep to face the reality of the day before him: he had to travel eighty kilometers with the troupe for afternoon and evening performances, and they had been expecting him at eight-thirty in the lobby of the hotel: once again the tour administrator would lose his temper and take him to task. How dreams come to an end!

Fabio dressed hastily, careful not to make any noise. It was the only way he could prolong the enchantment.

Before leaving the room, he went over to Donatella, abandoned on the vast four-poster bed. Pale, fine, so slender, a smile on her lips, she was still sleeping. Fabio did not have the heart to wake her. He said an imaginary goodbye, and, as he recalled, even went so far as to think he loved her, and would always love her; then he slipped away.

Now the bus was driving through the gates of the citadel,

taking the Green Snail Theatre Troupe to the municipal theater. The director climbed onto the bus and glumly announced that they had not sold more than a third of the seats. He seemed to blame them for it.

Fifteen years later, it was still true, what he had thought when taking his leave of Donatella . . . He loved her. Yes, he still loved her. Perhaps even more than ever.

The story had no ending. Perhaps it was for that reason that it endured.

He had left the citadel at a run, just in time to reach the hotel and close his suitcase; the theater manager had sent on the orchids from his dressing room. Fabio had jumped into his car—in those days, as leading man, he was entitled to a chauffeured limousine, not relegated to the bus with the rest of the troupe like today—he had fallen asleep again, then on waking swore to call the luxurious inn; but he had had to rehearse his cues and exits at the new theater, and perform, and rehearse again.

So he had postponed calling. Until he no longer dared to call. His everyday existence took over; it was as if he had dreamt it all; but above all as he revisited his memories he understood that Donatella had implied, more than once, that this was to be a unique event, as much for her as for him; a marvel with no tomorrow.

Why disturb her? She was rich, of high birth, no doubt already married. He resigned himself to the role she had given him: the whim of a single night. He thought with amusement that he had been an object for her, a plaything; he had taken great pleasure in incarnating her phantasm; and she had asked it of him with such kindness, such elegance . . .

The bus ceased its throbbing: they had arrived. The Green Snail Theatre Troupe would have two whole hours on their own before they were due to meet at the theater.

Fabio left his luggage in his tiny room, and headed for the inn.

As he wound his way up the hill, he thought of how ridiculous his hope was. Why was he imagining he might ever see her again? If she had been staying at that hotel back then, it was because she did not live here; she had given him no reason to think he might find her there today.

"I'm not really on my way to a rendezvous," he thought bitterly. "Any more than I'm conducting an investigation. I'm on a pilgrimage. I'm walking amongst my memories, memories of a time when I was young and handsome and famous, a time when a princess could desire me."

When he arrived at the inn, he was even more impressed than in the past, because at present he had a better understanding of the value of things: it would require a substantial income to stay in a place like this.

He hesitated before going through the door.

They'll kick me out. You can tell from the first glance that I don't have the means to pay for even a cocktail at the bar.

To find the necessary courage, he reminded himself that he was an actor, and that he had his looks: he decided to play the part, and went through the door.

At the reception, he avoided the younger employees and went over to the concierge, who must have been in his sixties, and who not only was more likely to have been working there fifteen years earlier, but might also have a concierge's sharp memory.

"Excuse me, I am Fabio Fabbri, I'm an actor, and I stayed here fifteen years ago. Were you here at the time?"

"Yes, sir. I was an elevator boy at the time. What can I do for you?"

"Well, there was a young woman staying here then, very beautiful, nobility. Do you remember her by any chance?"

"Many people of royal blood stay here, sir."

"She went by the name Donatella, although I doubt that . . . The personnel addressed her as 'Princess.'"

The man with the golden keys began to ruffle through his memories.

"Let's see, let's see, Princess Donatella, Princess Donatella . . . No, I'm sorry, sir, I don't recall."

"But you must remember her. In addition to the fact that she was very young and very beautiful, she was also rather eccentric. For example, she went around barefoot."

The detail seemed to ignite something in the man, and he delved into another niche of his memory before suddenly exclaiming, "Now I remember! It was Rosa!"

"Rosa?"

"Rosa Lombardi!"

"Rosa Lombardi. As I conjectured, Donatella was merely a name she had borrowed for the evening. Do you have any news of her? Does she still stay here on occasion? I must confess she is the sort of woman one does not easily forget."

The man sighed, and leaned on the counter as if speaking, now, to an acquaintance.

"Of course I remember her. Rosa . . . She worked here as a waitress. She was the daughter of the dishwasher in the kitchen, Pepino Lombardi. She was so young, poor child, when she was diagnosed with leukemia, you know, that blood disease . . . We all loved her so dearly. She made us feel so sorry for her that we tried in whatever ways we could to fulfill her desires until she went to die at the hospital. Poor thing, how old was she, eighteen maybe? From her earliest childhood she had gone around the village without her shoes. For a laugh we used to call her the barefoot princess . . ."

ODETTE TOULEMONDE

Calm down, Odette, calm down.

She felt so lively, impatient, and enthusiastic that it was as if she were taking flight, leaving the streets of Brussels behind, rising above the rows of facades, flying above the roofs to join the pigeons in the sky. Anyone who saw her light figure tearing down the Mont des Arts would surmise that this woman, with a feather in her curls, was singularly bird-like . . .

She was about to see him! For real . . . she would go up to him . . . even touch him, perhaps, if he shook her hand . . .

Calm down, Odette, calm down.

Although she was over forty, her heart was running away with her as if she were a teenage girl. Whenever a pedestrian crossing obliged her to wait on the pavement, she could feel a tingling in her thighs, and her ankles threatened to spring her forward; she would have liked to leap over the cars.

When she arrived at the bookstore, there was already a long line, as befitted a great day; she was told she would have to wait forty-five minutes before she could see him.

She grabbed the new book from the pyramid the booksellers had made with multiple copies—as fine as any Christmas tree—and began to read along with the other women who were waiting. They may all have been Balthazar Basan's readers, but not one of them could possibly be as assiduous, exact, and passionate as Odette.

"Well, you see, I've read all his books, absolutely everything, and loved every one," she said, as if apologizing for her erudition.

She felt very proud on discovering that she knew the author and his works better than anyone. Because her background was modest, because she worked as a shop assistant by day and a feather-maker by night, because she knew herself to be of mediocre intelligence, because she commuted by bus from Charleroi, an old mining town, she was nothing less than delighted to discover that among all these fine bourgeois ladies from Brussels she held a superior rank in the Balthazar Balsan fan club department.

In the middle of the store, enthroned upon a platform, illuminated by spotlights (nothing new to him, he was so used to the spotlights on television), Balthazar Balsan applied himself diligently and good-naturedly to the book signing. After twelve novels—all of them triumphs—he no longer knew whether he liked these signing sessions or not; on the one hand, he found it boring, such a repetitive and monotonous undertaking; on the other hand he enjoyed meeting his readers. These days, however, weariness prevailed over any appetite for conversation; he carried on more out of habit than desire, for he was at a difficult stage in his career where he no longer really needed to help with the sales of his books, but nevertheless feared that they might dwindle without him. And that the quality might suffer, as well . . . Could it be that with his latest opus he had just written the "one book too many," the one that was nothing special, the one that was not as vital as the others had been? For the time being he refused to allow doubt to contaminate him, for it was something he experienced with each new publication.

Among all the unfamiliar faces there was one that caught his attention, as she stood taller than all the others: a beautiful dark-skinned woman dressed in lustrous bronze raw silk, off to one side and striding back and forth on her own. Although she was absorbed by a telephone conversation, from time to time she looked over at the writer with a sparkling gaze.

"Who is that?" he asked the marketing director.

"Your publicist for Belgium. Would you like me to introduce you?"

"Please."

He was delighted to interrupt the signing for a few seconds, to take the hand that Florence held out to him.

"I'll be looking after you for a few days," she murmured, unsettled.

"I do hope so," he confirmed, with emphatic warmth.

The young woman's fingers responded favorably to the pressure of his palm, and a flicker of acknowledgment lit her eyes. Balthazar knew he had won: he would not be spending the night alone in his hotel.

Revived, already hungry for some sexual amusement, he turned toward the next reader with the smile of an ogre and asked in a vibrant voice, "Well, Madame, what can I do for you?"

Odette was so surprised by the virile energy with which he addressed her that she instantaneously lost all composure.

"Mmm . . . Mmm . . . Mmm . . ."

She could not utter a single word.

Balthazar Balsan looked at her without looking at her, friendly in a professional sort of way.

"Do you have a book with you?"

Odette didn't move, although she was clutching a copy of *Silence of the Plain* against her chest.

"Would you like me to sign the latest book?"

With a colossal effort, she managed to make a sign of acquiescence.

He reached out to take the book; misjudging, Odette stepped backwards, onto the toes of the lady behind her, understood her error, and suddenly thrust the book forward with a grand gesture that nearly swiped the author in the head.

"To whom shall I sign it?"

Silence.

"Is it for you?"

Odette nodded.

"What's your name?"

Odette just stood there.

"Your first name?"

Odette, deciding to risk her all, opened her mouth and murmured, swallowing furiously, "—dette!"

"Pardon?"

"—dette!"

"Dette?"

Increasingly unhappy, choking, on the verge of fainting, she tried one last time to articulate.

"—dette!"

A few hours later, sitting on a bench, as the light faded to gray and darkness rose from the ground to the sky, Odette could not bring herself to undertake her return journey to Charleroi. Disconcerted, she reread and reread the title page where her favorite author had inscribed, "For Dette."

There it was. She had botched her sole encounter with the writer of her dreams, and her children were going to make fun of her . . . And they would be right. Was there another woman on earth her age who was incapable of pronouncing her own name?

But as soon as she was on the bus, she forgot all about the incident and began to levitate. For from the very first sentence, Balthazar Balsan's new book drenched her in light and carried her away into his world, blotting out all her troubles, her shame, her neighbors' conversations, the sound of machines, and the dreary, industrial landscape of Charleroi. Thanks to Balthazar Balsan, she had her head in the clouds.

Once she was at home, she moved about on tiptoe not to

wake anyone—above all she did not want to be interrogated about her defeat—and she went to bed, propped up against her pillows, gazing at the panorama on the opposite wall which represented two shadow puppet lovers against a marine sunset. She could not tear herself away from the pages, and did not switch off her bedside lamp until she had finished the entire book.

As for Balthazar Balsan, he had a far more carnal night. The lovely Florence offered herself to him without ado, and in the presence of this black Venus with her perfect body he endeavored to be a good lover; so much ardor required a certain effort, and revealed painfully that he had also accumulated a certain fatigue on a sexual level; he was beginning to notice the price to be paid for certain things, and wondered whether, in spite of himself, he had not turned a corner where age was concerned.

At midnight, Florence wanted to switch on the television to watch a popular literary program, devoted that evening to Balthazar Balsan's new book. Balthazar would never have accepted had it not given him a chance to enjoy a restorative truce.

On the screen there appeared the face of the dreaded literary critic Olaf Pims, and some inexplicable instinct warned Balthazar Balsan that he was about to be attacked.

From behind his red eyeglasses—the glasses of the matador about to play with the bull, before going for the kill—the man looked bored, even downright disgusted.

"I have been asked to report on Balthazar Balsan's latest novel. So be it. If only we could be sure that it will also be his last, then that would be good news for us all! For I am absolutely aghast. From a literary point of view, this book is a disaster. Everything is cause for consternation—the story, the characters, the style . . . How can one be so consistently and unrelentingly bad from one book to the next: it is nothing short of an exploit close to genius. If it were possible to die of boredom, I would have died last night."

In his hotel room, naked with a towel around his waist, Balthazar Balsan watched open-mouthed the live broadcast of his own demolition. Next to him on the bed, Florence was embarrassed, and wriggled like a maggot trying to get back to the surface.

Olaf Pims tranquilly pursued his massacre.

"It pains me all the more to have to say this, because I have encountered Balthazar Balsan in a social context, and he is a likeable sort—kind, well-groomed, with the somewhat ridiculous physique of a high-school gym teacher, but in all respects he is the sort of individual one can associate with; in short, the kind of man with whom a woman can have a pleasant divorce."

With a little smile, Olaf Pims turned towards the camera and spoke as if he were suddenly addressing Balthazar Balsan himself.

"When one is so gifted at clichés, Monsieur Balsan, one does not call this a novel, but a dictionary, yes, a dictionary of platitudes, a dictionary of hollow statements. In the meantime, here is what your book deserves: the garbage can, and as quickly as possible."

Olaf Pims tore up the copy of the book he had been holding and tossed it scornfully behind him. Balthazar felt his gesture like an uppercut.

On the set, shocked by such a violent reaction, the presenter asked, "Well, then, how do you explain his success?"

"Simple-minded people are entitled to their heroes, too. I do not doubt that concierges, supermarket checkers, hairdressers, and the like who collect dolls at the county fair or photos of sunsets have found in Balthazar Balsan their ideal author."

Florence switched off the television and turned to Balthazar. If she had been a more experienced publicist, she would have dished up the usual objections for situations like this: the man is bitter, and cannot stand to see that your books are in fashion; he reads them and assumes you're soliciting readers; consequently, he sees anything that is simply natural as demagogy, finds commercial interest beneath technical virtuosity, and brands your desire to offer something interesting to readers as marketing; moreover, he defeats his own argument by treating your audience as an unworthy subhuman species, and his scorn for society is downright staggering. However, because she was young, Florence remained malleable; her intelligence was mediocre, and she mistook nastiness for critical savvy; for her, consequently, the die was cast.

It was no doubt because he felt the young women's scornful, pitying gaze on his person that Balthazar, that night, entered a stage of depression. He had always had his share of bad-tempered remarks, but as for eyes full of pity, never. He began to feel like an old, ridiculous has-been.

In the meantime, Odette had reread *Silence of the Plain* three times, and considered it to be one of Balthazar Balsan's best books to date. She eventually related her botched encounter with the writer to her son Rudy, a hairdresser. Careful not to laugh, he understood that his mother was unhappy.

"What did you expect? What did you want to say to him?"

"That not only are his books good, they are good for me. The best anti-depressants on earth. They should be covered by health plans."

"Well, since you didn't manage to tell him in person, all you have to do is write him a letter."

"You don't think that would be a little weird, me writing to a writer?"

"Why would it be weird?"

"A woman who's so bad at writing, writing to a man who's so good at writing?"

"Well, bald hairdressers exist, don't they?!"

Persuaded by Rudy's reasoning, she sat down in the living room-dining room, put away her feather projects, and wrote her letter.

Dear Monsieur Balsan,

I never write, because even if I can spell, I'm no poet. And I'd need to be a really good poet to tell you how important you are to me. In fact, I owe you my life. Without you I would have done myself in twenty times. You see how badly I write? One time would be enough!

I have only ever loved one man, my husband Antoine. He is still as handsome, slim, and young as ever. It's incredible, never to change like that. Well, fact is he's been dead for ten years, so that helps. I haven't wanted to replace him. That's my way of going on loving him.

So I brought up my two children, Sue Helen and Rudy, on my own.

Rudy's turned out all right, I think: he's a hairdresser and he earns his living, he's a cheerful boy and kind, too; he tends to change his friends a bit too often but hey, he's only nineteen, he's having fun.

Sue Helen is another story. She's the gloomy sort. She was born with her hair standing on end. Even at night in her dreams she complains. She's going out with a real jerk, a sort of ape who spends all day fiddling with mopeds but never brings home a dime. For the last two years he's been living with us. And on top of it, he's got this problem: his feet stink.

To be honest, my life, before I started reading you, well, I thought it was pretty ugly, ugly like a Sunday afternoon in Charleroi when the sky is low, ugly like a washing machine that quits on you just when you need it, ugly like an empty bed. At night, on a regular basis, I felt like swallowing a bunch of sleeping tablets to get it over with. Then one day I read your book. It was as if someone had drawn the curtains and let in the light. In your books you show how in every life, no matter how miserable, there are reasons to be happy, to laugh, to love. You show that little people like me actually deserve a lot of credit because everything costs them so much more than other people. Thanks to your books, I learned how to respect myself. Even to like myself a bit. I've become the Odette Toulemonde people know today: a woman who opens her shutters every morning with pleasure and closes them again every evening with pleasure.

Someone should have injected your books intravenously in me after Antoine died, it would have saved me a lot of time.

When one day, as late as possible I hope, you go to Paradise, God will come up to you and say, "There are a lot of people who want to thank you for the good you did on earth, Monsieur Balsan," and among those millions of people there'll be me, Odette Toulemonde. Odette Toulemonde, please forgive her, was too impatient to wait for that moment.

Odette

No sooner had she finished than Rudy swept out of his room, where he'd been flirting with his new little boyfriend; they were in such a hurry to run out and tell Odette the news that they had barely taken the time to throw on a pair of boxers and a shirt. According to the Internet, Balthazar Balsan was going to give another signing very soon, in Namur, not far from there.

"So you'll be able to hand him your letter in person!"

Balthazar Balsan did not come on his own to the bookstore in Namur; his publisher had joined him from Paris to lend him moral support, and this fact merely depressed him further.

If my publisher is spending a few days with me, it means things are really bad, he figured.

Indeed, like wolves, critics travel in packs; Olaf Pims's attack had unleashed them. Those who up to now had withheld their grievances or indifference with regard to Balthazar Balsan now let it all out; those who had never even read him still voiced resentment against his success; and those who had no opinion spoke about him as well, because they had to join the fray.

Balthazar Balsan felt incapable of responding: this was not his playing field. He could not play offensively, he lacked aggression; he had become a novelist for no reason other than to extol life, in its beauty and complexity. If he were to become indignant, it should surely be for the sake of a worthy cause, not his own. His only reaction was to suffer and wait for it all to blow over—unlike his publisher, who would have liked to make the most of the fuss in the media.

In Namur the readers were not as numerous as in Brussels: in just a few days, it had become "dépassé" to like Balthazar Balsan. So the author was even more amiable with those who did venture up to him.

Unaware of all the fuss, since she did not read the papers or watch the cultural programs, Odette could not imagine that her writer was going through such dark hours. Dolled up, but not as chic as the first time, heartened by the glass of white wine that Rudy had forced her to imbibe in the café across the street, she came up to Balthazar Balsan all aquiver.

"Hello, do you recognize me?"

"Uh . . . yes . . . we met . . . let's see . . . last year . . . Help me on this . . ."

Not the least bit put out, Odette was actually glad that he'd forgotten her ridiculous performance on the previous Tuesday, so she released him from his scrambling effort to pretend to remember.

"No, I was joking. We've never met."

"Ah, that's what I thought, otherwise I'd have remembered. To whom have I the honor?"

"Toulemonde. Odette Toulemonde."

"Pardon?"

"Toulemonde, that's my name."

When he heard her comical last name, Balthazar thought she must be joking.

"You're having me on?"

"Pardon?"

Realizing his gaffe, Balthazar corrected himself.

"Well, tell me, it's a rather original name . . ."

"Not in my family!"

Odette handed him a new volume to inscribe.

"Could you just write, 'For Odette'?"

Balthazar, distracted, wanted to be certain he had heard correctly.

"Odette?"

"Yes, my parents really got me there!"

"What do you mean, Odette is a lovely name . . ."

"It's dreadful!"

"No."

"Yes!"

"It's Proustian."

"Prou—?"

"Proustian. *Remembrance of Things Past . . .* Odette de Crécy, the woman Swann is in love with . . ."

"The only creatures I know who are called Odette are poodles. Yes, poodles. And me. And with me, everyone forgets my name. Maybe to make them remember, I should put on a collar and get my hair curled?"

He examined her, not sure he'd heard correctly, then burst out laughing.

Leaning toward him, Odette handed him an envelope.

"Here, this is for you. When I talk to you, nothing but nonsense comes out of my mouth, so I wrote you a letter."

Odette fled, in a rustling of feathers.

*

When he had settled into the rear seat of the car that was taking him back to Paris with his publisher, Balthazar had a passing urge to read Odette's message; but when he saw the kitsch paper, a weave of pink garlands and lilac branches held by cherubs with plump buttocks, he decided not to open it. There was no way round it, Olaf Pims was right: he wrote for hairdressers and supermarket checkers, and he simply had the audience he deserved. With a sigh, he slipped the letter inside his camel's hair coat.

A descent into hell awaited him in Paris. Not only did his wife—evasive, absorbed by her law practice—fail to show the least little sign of compassion for what he was going through, his ten-year-old son got into fights at the lycée with little squirts who were making fun of his father. There were few messages of sympathy, and never from the literary milieu—perhaps that was his fault, he did not frequent it. Shut away inside his huge apartment on the Île Saint-Louis, next to a telephone that did not ring—that was his fault, too, he never gave out his number—he took an objective look at his life and suspected that he had made a mess of it.

To be sure, he had a beautiful wife, but Isabelle was cold, curt, ambitious, rich through inheritance, far more used to moving in a world of predators than he was—and had they not agreed to allow extramarital affairs, a sure sign that it was social cement that held their couple together more than any ties of love? To be sure, he owned an apartment in the center of Paris which left many people feeling envious, but did he really like it? There was nothing on the walls, windows, shelves, or sofas that he himself had chosen: a decorator had done it all. In the living room there was a grand piano that no one played, a laughable symbol of social rank; his study had been designed with magazine publication in mind, because Balthazar actually preferred to write in cafés. He realized he was living in a décor. Worse than that—a décor that wasn't even of his own making.

And what had he done with his money? He'd used it to show that he had arrived, that he was established in a class he had not been born into . . . Nothing that he possessed truly enriched him, although everything he owned suggested wealth.

While he was vaguely aware of this inconsistency, it never made him ill, because Balthazar was saved by the faith he placed in his own work. And now even that was under attack . . . He began to have his doubts. Had he written even one worthy novel? Was jealousy the only motivation for such acid critiques? And what if those who condemned him were right?

Fragile, emotional, used to maintaining his equilibrium in creativity, he found that in real life he could not attain it. It was unbearable to him that his ongoing interior debate—is my actual talent up to the level I would like?—had become public. So public, in fact, that one evening, after a kindly soul had pointed out that Balthazar's wife was associating assiduously with Olaf Pims, he tried to commit suicide.

When the Filipino maid found him lying there lifeless, it was not too late. The emergency services managed to revive him and then, after a few days under observation, he was sent to a psychiatric hospital.

There, he shut himself away in a healing silence. And there, no doubt, he would eventually, after a few weeks, have responded to the valiant and caring psychiatrists who were trying to deliver him, had the untimely arrival of his wife not altered the course of his treatment.

When he heard the metallic slam of car doors closing, he hardly needed to look out the window to ascertain that it was indeed Isabelle who was parking her tank in the lot. In a split second he gathered his things, grabbed his coat, shoved open the door leading onto the external stairway, checked to see as he hurried down the stairs that he did indeed have a double of all the keys, rushed over to Isabelle's car, and switched on the ignition while she was taking the elevator.

He drove aimlessly for several kilometers, exhausted. Where should he go? It hardly mattered. Every time he pictured himself finding refuge with someone, the moment he knew he would have to provide an explanation, he gave up on the idea.

He stopped at a freeway rest area, and was stirring his sugary coffee with its savor of paper cup, when he noticed a thickness in the pocket of his camel's hair coat.

For lack of anything better to do, he opened the letter, and sighed: as if the bad taste of the paper were not enough, his fan had added to her missive a red felt heart embroidered with feathers. He began skimming through the letter; by the time he had finished it he was in tears.

When one day, as late as possible I hope, you go to Paradise, God will come up to you and say, "There are a lot of people who want to thank you for the good you did on earth, Monsieur Balsan," and among those millions of people there'll be me, Odette Toulemonde. Odette Toulemonde, please forgive her, was too impatient to wait for that moment.

When he reckoned he had made the most of their comforting effect, he switched on the ignition and decided to seek out the author of those pages.

That evening Odette Toulemonde was preparing an *île flottante*, the favorite dessert of her ferocious daughter Sue Helen, a post-adolescent burdened with a dental retainer who went from one job interview to another without ever being hired. She was beating the egg whites into peaks, humming to herself, when someone rang at the door. Annoyed at being interrupted during such a delicate procedure, Odette hastily wiped her hands, did not bother to cover the simple nylon petticoat she was wearing and, certain that it must be a neighbor from the same floor, went to open the door.

She stood there with her mouth open, gaping at Balthazar Balsan, who was weak, exhausted, and unshaven, a travel bag in his hand. He was staring at her feverishly, brandishing an envelope.

"Are you the person who wrote this letter?"

Confused, Odette thought he was going to tell her off.

"Yes, but . . ."

"Ah, I found you," he said, with a sigh of relief.

Odette stood there, speechless.

"I have only one question to ask you," he continued, "and I'd like for you to answer."

"Yes?"

"Do you love me?"

"Yes."

She had not hesitated.

For him, this was a precious moment, an instant he could savor to the full. He did not think for a moment about how it might embarrass Odette.

Odette, distraught and rubbing her hands, did not dare broach the subject of her concern; but in the end she could not restrain herself.

"My egg whites . . ."

"I beg your pardon?"

"The problem is, I was beating my egg whites and you know, egg whites, if you wait too long, they . . ."

At a loss, she made a gesture to describe the deflating surrender of egg whites.

Balthazar Balsan was too upset to grasp what she meant.

"In fact, I have another question."

"Yes?"

"May I ask you?"

"Yes."

"Really, may I?"

"Yes."

Looking down at the floor without meeting her gaze, like a guilty child, he asked, "Would it be possible to stay with you for a few days?"

"Sorry?"

"Just answer, yes or no?"

Odette, overwhelmed, thought for a few seconds then exclaimed, as natural as could be, "Yes. But hurry, please, my egg whites!"

She grabbed his travel bag and pulled Balthazar inside.

And that is how Balthazar Balsan, without anyone in Paris suspecting a thing, settled in Charleroi in the home of Odette Toulemonde, shop assistant by day and feather-maker by night.

"Feather-maker?" he asked, one evening.

"I sew feathers on dancer's costumes. You know, for variety shows, Folies-Bergères, Casino de Paris, that sort of thing . . . it helps to make ends meet, with what I make at the store."

Balthazar was discovering a life as different from his own as could be imagined: a life with neither glory nor money, but where, still, there was happiness.

Odette had a talent: joy. In her deepest self, it was as if there were a non-stop jazz band playing lively tunes, pulsating melodies. No hardship seemed to get her down. When faced with a problem, she looked for the solution. Since humility and modesty were part of her personality, no matter what the circumstances she did not stop to think that she might deserve better, and consequently she rarely felt frustrated. Thus, when talking to Balthazar about the brick apartment block where she lived with other welfare tenants, she referred only to the small balconies painted in summery ice cream pastels and decorated with plastic flowers, or the hallways adorned with macramé and geraniums and drawings of sailors holding their pipes.

"When you're lucky enough to live here, you don't want to move. You only leave this place feet first in a pine box . . . It's a little paradise, this apartment block!"

She was well disposed toward all humankind, and was able to remain on good terms with people who considered themselves her exact opposite, because she did not judge them. Take her own hallway: she was friendly with an orange Flemish couple who were sunbed freaks and swingers; she fraternized with a brittle, peremptory town employee who knew everything about everything; she exchanged recipes with a young junkie who already had five children and was subject to fits of rage during which she would scratch the walls; and she bought meat and bread for a Monsieur Wilpute, an impotent, racist pensioner, on the pretext that "he may well spout a lot of nonsense," but he was still a human being.

With her family, she was equally open-minded: her son Rudy's unbridled homosexuality was less troubling to her than Sue Helen's gloominess. Gently, despite the fact she was rebuffed from morning to night, she tried to help her daughter smile, to learn patience, to keep faith and, if possible, to dump her boyfriend Polo, that dumb gluttonous smelly parasite, whom Rudy referred to as "the lump."

They took Balthazar into their crowded household, and no one asked him any bothersome questions; it was as if he were some cousin passing through, to whom hospitality was naturally owed. He could not help but compare this welcome with his own attitude—or his wife's—whenever friends asked to stay with them in Paris. "And what's the point of hotels, then!" Isabelle would exclaim each time, furious, before suggesting to the impolite beggars that they would be so cramped that everyone would feel uncomfortable.

Because no one questioned his presence, Balthazar did not wonder, either, what he was doing there, or even less why he stayed on. For as long as any explanation was spared him, he was able to recover his strength, and he did not even know himself to what degree this social and cultural change of scene was taking him back to his origins. Abandoned by his mother at birth, he had been raised by different foster families, all of modest means, kind people who for several years would take in an orphan along with their own children. As a very young boy he had sworn he would "escape through the top" by excelling in his studies: his true identity would be intellectual. With the help of scholarships, he learned Greek, Latin, English, German, and Spanish; he raided the public libraries in order to acquire some culture; he prepared, and passed, the entrance examinations to one of the best schools in France and added a few university degrees along the way. His academic prowess should have led him to a conformist sort of profession—university professor or attaché in a ministerial cabinet—had he not in the meanwhile discovered his talent for writing and decided to devote himself to it entirely. Oddly, in his books he did not describe the milieu to which he belonged since he had risen in society, but the one in which he had spent his earliest years: this no doubt explained the harmony of his work, his success with the common people, and the disdain of the intelligentsia. Becoming a member of the Toulemonde family took him back to simple pleasures, to considerations that were devoid of ambition, to the pure pleasure of living among warm-hearted people.

One day when talking with the neighbors, he found out that everyone in the building assumed he was Odette's lover.

When he insisted to Filip, the swinger neighbor who had set up a body-building gym in his garage, that he wasn't, Filip begged him not to take him for a fool.

"Odette hasn't had a man round her place in years. And you know, I totally understand you: there's no harm in having some fun! She's a good-looking gal, is Odette. If she said yes to me, I wouldn't say no."

Disconcerted, sensing that it wouldn't be right to keep protesting to the contrary, Balthazar went back to the apartment with some new questions to mull over.

"Do I desire her without realizing it? I've never thought about it. She's not my type of woman . . . she's too . . . I don't know . . . well, no, not at all . . . And she's my age . . . if I were going to desire someone, she'd have to be younger, normally . . . At the same time, nothing is normal around here. And what am I doing here, after all?"

That evening the kids had gone to a pop concert and he found himself alone with Odette, and looked at her through different eyes.

In the subdued light of the street lamp, comely in her angora sweater, busy sewing a set of feathers onto a sequined fabric, she looked very cute. Something he had totally failed to notice until now.

Maybe Filip is right . . . why hadn't it occurred to me?

Sensing she was being observed, Odette raised her head and smiled at him. The awkwardness vanished.

To get closer to her, he put down his book and served the coffee.

"Do you have a dream, Odette?"

"Yes . . . to go to the sea."

"The Mediterranean?"

"Why the Mediterranean? We have the sea here, too, maybe it's not as beautiful but it's more discreet, more reserved . . . the North Sea, that's what it is."

He sat down next to her to take another cup of coffee, and he let his head slide onto her shoulder. She quivered. Encouraged, he let his fingers wander along her arm, her shoulder, her neck. She trembled. Finally, he brought his lips closer.

"No. Please."

"Don't you like me?"

"Don't be silly . . . of course I do . . . but, no."

"Antoine? Are you thinking of Antoine?"

Odette lowered her gaze, dried a tear, and declared, very sadly, as if she were betraying her late husband, "No. It isn't because of Antoine."

Balthazar concluded that the path was clear, and he planted his lips on Odette's.

A resounding slap burned his cheek. Then, in utter contradiction, Odette's fingers rushed to his face to stroke him, to erase the slap.

"Oh, forgive me, forgive me."

"I don't understand. Don't you want . . ."

"To hurt you? Oh no, forgive me."

"Don't you want to sleep with me?"

A second slap was Odette's answer and then, horrified, she sprang from the sofa, fled from the living room, and ran to lock herself in her bedroom.

The following day, after a night spent in Filip's garage, Balthazar decided to leave, to avoid sinking any further into an absurd situation. Already headed down the freeway, he nevertheless made a detour by the hairdresser's salon where Rudy worked, in order to slip him a wad of bank notes.

"I have to go back to Paris. Your mother is tired, and she dreams of going to the sea. Take this money and rent a house there, won't you? But above all, don't tell her it was me. Just say you received some sort of bonus. Okay?"

Without waiting for Rudy's reply, Balthazar jumped in his car.

In Paris, the situation had improved during his absence, for people were already talking about other things. His publisher was confident that, with time, Balthazar would regain the faith of his readers and the media.

To avoid running into his wife, he went by the house very quickly, at a time when he knew she would be at work; he left her a note to reassure her about his present state—did she even care, anyway?—and he packed a suitcase before heading off to Savoie, where his son was at ski camp with his class.

I'll manage to find a room somewhere in the area, he thought.

The minute father and son were reunited, François no longer wanted his dad to leave. After several days of skiing together, Balthazar realized that, as an absent father, he had an enormous amount of catching up to do with his child, in terms of presence, and love.

Moreover, he couldn't help but notice that his son showed signs of the same chronic fragility and anxiety that Balthazar himself was plagued with. By acting like other people, François hoped they would accept him, but at the same time he suffered from not being his own self.

"Since Easter vacation will soon be here, how would you like to go to the sea? Just the two of us?"

In reply, the boy jumped in his arms, shrieking with joy.

On Easter Sunday, Odette found herself looking out at the North Sea for the first time. Intimidated, she sketched drawings in the sand. The vastness of the water, the sky, the beach, all seemed a luxury beyond her means; it was as if she were partaking of a splendor to which she had no right.

Suddenly, she felt a burning sensation on her neck, and found herself thinking intensely about Balthazar. When she turned around, there he stood, on the dike, holding his son by the hand.

They were overjoyed to see each other again, but cautiously gentle, fearful of hurting one another.

"I came to find you, Odette, because my son needs lessons. Are you still giving them?"

"What?"

"Lessons in happiness?"

Balthazar and his son moved in to the rented cabin as if their presence there was perfectly natural, and their vacation got off to a start.

When life had settled into a rhythm, Odette decided to explain to Balthazar why she had slapped him.

"I don't want to sleep with you, because I know I won't be living with you. You're just passing through my life. You came into it, and then you left again."

"I've come back."

"You'll leave again. I'm not a fool: there is no shared future in store for Balthazar Balsan, great Parisian writer, and Odette Toulemonde, shop assistant from Charleroi. It's too late. If we were twenty years younger, perhaps . . ."

"Age has nothing to do with—"

"It does. Age means that our lives are more behind us than ahead of us, that you've settled into one way of life and me into another. Paris-Charleroi, money-no money: the die is cast. Our paths may cross, but we can no longer meet each other."

Balthazar wasn't really sure what he expected from Odette; but he needed her, that much he knew.

Where everything else was concerned, their affair was not really much of one. Perhaps she was right to keep him from heading into the banality of a love affair? But what if she were wrong . . . Was she not depriving herself of her body? Had she not been inflicting a sort of senseless widowhood on herself ever since Antoine died?

This became particularly apparent one evening when they started dancing in the fisherman's cabin. Giving her all to the samba, Odette moved in a sensual, gracious, mischievous way, revealing a saucy, insolent femininity that Balthazar would never even have suspected her of. In that brief moment, Balthazar took a few steps around her and sensed, as their shoulders touched and their hips grazed, that he could very easily end up in bed with her.

In the moonlight, she made an ingenuous confession:

"You know, Balthazar, I'm not in love with you."

"Oh?"

"No. I'm not in love with you; I love you."

He thought her declaration was the most beautiful one he had ever heard—more beautiful even than the ones he invented in his books.

In reply, he handed her the lizard-skin file that contained the new novel he had been writing since his arrival at the seaside.

"It will be called *Other People's Happiness.* I'm going to tell the story of several characters who are searching for happiness without finding it. If they fail, it's because they've been given or they've adopted ideas about happiness that don't suit them: money, power, a good marriage, mistresses with long legs, racing cars, huge duplex apartments in Paris, chalets in Megève and villas in Saint Tropez, nothing but clichés. They may be successful but they're not happy, because what they are experiencing is other people's happiness, happiness according to other people. I owe this book to you. Read the beginning."

By the light of the lantern she read the first page. He had written, "To Dette."

She felt so light that it was as if the crown of her head were touching the moon. Her heart was nearly breaking. Taking a breath, she lifted her hand to her heart and murmured, "Calm down, Odette, calm down."

At midnight they kissed on the cheek, wishing each other sweet dreams, but Balthazar envisioned that by the end of the two days they had left at the seaside they would, logically, have become lovers.

An unpleasant surprise awaited him when he came back from his bike ride with François, Rudy, and Sue Helen. His wife and his publisher were waiting patiently in the living room.

When he saw Isabelle, he suspected she was up to no good, and he nearly lost his temper with her. Odette calmed him down.

"Don't be angry with her. I'm the one who arranged this meeting, on my own. Sit down and help yourself to a piece of cake. It's homemade. I'm going to get us something to drink."

To Balthazar, the scene that followed was surreal. Trapped in a nightmare, Balthazar felt like he was watching Odette as Miss Marple at the close of an investigation: all the characters in the detective story were summoned, and over tea and crumpets Miss Marple explained the matter and drew her conclusions.

"Balthazar Balsan has brought me a great deal through his books. I never thought I would be able to repay him in any way until, through a combination of circumstances, he came to find refuge in my home some weeks ago. Soon he will have to go back to Paris, because at his age, and with his fame, you don't start your life over in Charleroi. But for the time being he doesn't dare, because he's ashamed, for one thing, but above all because he is afraid."

She turned toward Isabelle who looked skeptical at her use of the word "afraid."

"Afraid of you, Madame? Why should he be afraid of you? Because you don't admire him enough. You must be proud of your husband: he makes thousands of people happy. Maybe among all those readers there are little secretaries and insignificant employees like me—but that is precisely why! The fact that he can fascinate us, and move us, people like us who don't read a lot, who aren't cultured like yourself: well, that proves that he has more talent than all the others! Much more. Because you know, Madame, maybe that Olaf Pims writes magnificent books, too, but I would need a dictionary and more than one tube of aspirin just to figure out what on earth he's talking about. He's a snob who only writes for people who've read as many books as he has."

She handed a cup of tea to the publisher, training an angry gaze upon him.

"As for you, Monsieur, you must do more to defend your author against those people in Paris who insult him and give him the blues. When you're fortunate enough to be in the company of a treasure like Balthazar Balsan, you look after him. Or else you ought to change your profession, Monsieur. Taste my lemon sponge, I made it especially for the occasion!"

Terrified, the publisher obeyed. Odette turned once again to Isabelle Balsan.

"Are you thinking he doesn't love you? Or doesn't love you anymore? Maybe that's what he thinks, too . . . But I noticed something, I did: your photo, he has it on him all the time."

Isabelle, touched by Odette's simplicity, lowered her head.

"He's been so unfaithful to me . . ."

"Oh, if you think that a man isn't supposed to flirt with other women and sniff around elsewhere, you shouldn't have a man, Madame, you should have a dog! And even then you'd have to keep it chained to its doghouse. My Antoine, who I loved so much, and still love, twenty years later, I knew perfectly well that he'd left his paw prints on other women, who were different—maybe they were prettier, or maybe they just had a different smell. Whatever: he died in my arms. In my arms. Looking at me. And that will be a gift to me, forever."

She struggled for a moment with the emotion that came over her unexpectedly, and then forced herself to continue:

"Balthazar Balsan will come back to you. I've done the best I could to fix him up, to get him back in shape for you so that he'll smile and laugh, because, frankly, men like this one, so good and so gifted, so awkward, so generous, you can't let them drown. Two days from now I'll be headed back to Charleroi, back to the store. So I don't want my hard work to go to waste . . ."

Balthazar gazed painfully at Odette. She was tearing their

love affair to bits, and in public. He was angry at her, he hated her for inflicting this upon him. He thought that there was something lost and confused about her expression, as if she had gone crazy, but he felt it was pointless to try and protest. If she had decreed that this was the way things were to be, then there would be no budging her.

Before setting off again, he went for a walk in the dunes with Isabelle. Neither of them was convinced that they'd be able to live together again but, for François's sake, they agreed to give it a try.

When they came back to the fisherman's cabin, an ambulance hurtled past them, siren shrieking: Odette had just had a heart attack.

As long as her life was still hanging by a thread, everyone stayed in Blieckenbleck. Once the intensive care unit confirmed that Odette was out of danger, the publisher and Isabelle and her son returned to Paris.

Balthazar, on the other hand, arranged to prolong rental of the cabin; he kept an eye on Rudy and Sue Helen, stipulating that they must hide from their mother the fact he had stayed on.

"Later . . . when she's feeling better."

Every day, he took her children to the clinic and waited for them on a chair among the potted plants, grannies in bathrobes, and patients wandering around with their IVs hanging from poles.

Odette eventually regained her strength, her wits, and some color on her cheeks, and she was surprised to find that someone had put Antoine's photograph on her night table.

"Who put this here?"

The children confessed that the initiative had been Balthazar's and that he had stayed on in Blieckenbleck, taking care of them the way a father would.

Given their mother's emotion and the crazed reaction of the electrocardiogram, with its frenetic dance of green squiggles marking the rhythm of her palpitations, the children understood that Balthazar had been right to wait for her convalescence, and they wondered if her initial malaise was not due to her rejection of Balthazar: her heart had simply not been able to bear it.

The next morning Balthazar, as nervous as if he were fifteen years old, came into Odette's room. He offered her two bouquets.

"Why two?"

"One from me. One from Antoine."

"Antoine?"

Balthazar sat down by her bed and gently indicated her husband's photograph.

"We've become very good friends, Antoine and I. He's accepted me. He thinks that I love you well enough to have earned his respect. When you had your attack, he confessed that he'd been glad of it rather too hastily; he thought you were about to join him. Then he was angry with himself for having had such a selfish idea: now, for you and your children, he feels reassured that you are much better."

"What else did he say?"

"You're not going to like it . . ."

Balthazar leaned respectfully over toward Odette and murmured, "He has placed you in my trust . . ."

Deeply moved, Odette began to sob in silence. But then she tried to make a joke.

"He didn't ask for my opinion?"

"Antoine? No. He said you're the very stubborn sort."

He leaned over further still and added, with irresistible tenderness, "I told him . . . that it was fine with me."

And they kissed, at last.

The electrocardiogram immediately began to jiggle, and an

alarm went off, an urgent summons to the nursing staff: a heart was running away.

Balthazar removed his lips from hers and murmured, as he looked at her, "Calm down, Odette; calm down."

THE MOST BEAUTIFUL
BOOK IN THE WORLD

A shiver of hope went through them when they first saw Olga.

To be sure, she did not seem particularly kind. Tall, dry, with a prominent jawbone, jutting elbows, and sallow skin, when she first came in she did not look at a single woman in the ward. She sat down on the wobbly bunk she'd been assigned, put away her belongings at the bottom of the wooden chest, listened to the guard shouting the rules at her as if the latter were braying Morse code, did not turn her head until she was informed of the location of the washroom, and then, once the guard had left, she stretched out on her back, cracked her knuckles, and gave herself over to the contemplation of the blackened planks on the ceiling.

"Have you seen her hair?" murmured Tatyana.

The prisoners did not understand what Tatyana meant by that.

The newcomer had a thick mane of hair—frizzy, robust, coarse, which doubled the volume of her head. Such health and vigor—the sort of thing you usually only saw on the head of an African woman. But Olga, despite her olive skin, did not look remotely African, and must have come from somewhere in the Soviet Union, since here she was now in Siberia, in this women's camp where the regime punished those who did not think in the orthodox fashion.

"What about her hair, then?"

"I think she's from the Caucasus."

"You're right. Their women often have straw-like hair."

"Yes, horrible hair, isn't it."

"Not at all! It's magnificent! With my flat, fine hair, I could only dream of having hair like that."

"I'd rather die. It looks like horsehair."

"No—pubic hair!"

Giggling, quickly stifled, accompanied Lily's last remark.

Tatyana frowned and silenced the group by pointing out: "Her hair might offer us the solution."

Eager to please Tatyana, whom they treated as their leader even though she was just an ordinary prisoner like the others, they tried to concentrate on what they had failed to grasp: how could a stranger's hair offer any solution to the lives they were leading—that of political deviants being forcibly re-educated?

That night a thick snowfall had buried the camp. Outside, everything was dark except for the lantern that the storm was doing its best to extinguish. The temperature, well below zero, did not help them to concentrate.

"Do you mean . . ."

"Yes. I mean you can hide quite a few things in a head of hair like that."

They observed a moment of respectful silence. One of them finally guessed: "With her she has brought a . . ."

"Yes!"

Lily, a gentle blond woman who, despite the climate, the rigors of work, and the deplorable food, was still as round as any kept woman, now voiced a certain skepticism.

"Well, she'll have to have thought of it first."

"Why would she not have?"

"Well I certainly wouldn't have thought of it before coming here."

"And I'm referring to her, not to you."

Well aware that Tatyana would always have the final word,

Lily refrained from voicing her annoyance, and went back to sewing the hem of her woolen skirt.

They listened to the icy howling of the storm.

Leaving her companions behind, Tatyana went down the row, approached the foot of the newcomer's bed, and stood there for a while, waiting for a sign that would indicate she had been noticed.

A feeble flame was dying in the stove.

After a few minutes, during which she obtained no reaction, Tatyana resolved to break the silence: "What's your name?"

A deep voice answered, "Olga"; her lips had not moved.

"And why are you here?"

No reaction on Olga's face. A mask of wax.

"I expect, like all of us, you were Stalin's favorite fiancée and he got bored with you?"

She thought she was saying something funny, an almost ritual witticism that greeted all the opponents to the Stalinist regime; her words slid over the stranger like a pebble over ice.

"My name's Tatyana. Would you like me to introduce the others?"

"There'll be time enough for that, no?"

"There certainly will . . . we'll be in this hole for months, or years . . . we might even die here."

"So we have time."

To conclude, Olga closed her eyes and turned to face the wall, leaving only her angular shoulders to carry on the conversation.

Realizing she would get nothing more out of her, Tatyana went back to join the others.

"A tough nut. Which is reassuring. There's a chance that . . ."

Nodding approvingly, even Lily, they decided to wait.

In the week that followed, the newcomer offered up no more than a sentence a day, and even that had to be forced out of her. Such behavior seemed to validate the hopes of the old-est prisoners.

"I'm sure she's thought about it," said Lily eventually, more convinced with each passing hour. "She is definitely the type who would think about it."

The day brought little light. The fog forced its grayness upon it, and when it lifted, an impenetrable screen of oppressive clouds weighed upon the camp, like an army of sentinels.

As no one had been able to inspire Olga's trust, the women counted on the shower to show them whether the newcomer was hiding a . . . But it was so cold that no one attempted, anymore, to get undressed; so impossible would it be to get dry and warm after such an undertaking that everyone resorted to a furtive, minimal scrub. One rainy morning they discovered, moreover, that Olga's mane was so thick that the drops slid over it without adhering; her hair was waterproof.

"Never mind," ventured Tatyana, "we'll have to take the risk."

"Of asking her?"

"No. Of showing her."

"And what if she's a spy? What if she's been sent here to trap us?"

"She's not the type," said Tatyana.

"No, she's not the type at all," confirmed Lily, pulling on a thread in her sewing.

"Yes, she is the type! She's playing silent, tough, unfriendly, the sort who won't get close to anyone: isn't that the very best way to make us trust her?"

It was Irina who was vociferating in this manner, surprising the other women, surprising her own self, stupefied by the coherence of her reasoning. Astonished, she went on: "I can just imagine that if someone entrusted me with spying on a hut full of women, there would be no better way to go about it. Pass myself off as the quiet, solitary sort and, over time, gain the others' trust. That's cleverer than acting friendly, no? We may have been infiltrated by the biggest tattletale in the Soviet Union."

Lily was suddenly so convinced of this that she rammed her needle into the thick of her finger. A drop of blood formed, and she looked at it, terrified.

"I want to be moved into another hut, quick!"

Tatyana intervened.

"I understand your reasoning, Irina, but that's all it is, reasoning. As for me, my intuition tells me the opposite. We can trust her, she's like us. Or even harder than we are."

"Let's wait. Because if we are caught . . ."

"Yes, you're right. Let's wait. And above all, let's try to push her to the breaking point. Let's stop talking to her. If she's a spy who's been planted here to inform on us, she'll panic and try to get closer to us. With every step she takes she'll reveal her strategy."

"Good point," confirmed Irina. "Let's ignore her and see how she reacts."

"It's dreadful . . ." sighed Lily, licking her finger to speed the scarring.

For ten days, not one prisoner in ward 13 said a word to Olga. At first she didn't seem to notice and then, once she was aware of it, her gaze grew harder, almost mineral; and yet she did not make the slightest gesture to break the wall of silence. She accepted her isolation.

After they had had their soup, the women gathered around Tatyana.

"There's our proof, no? She didn't crack."

"Yes, it's terrifying."

"Oh, Lily, everything terrifies you."

"You have to admit it's a nightmare: to be rejected by the group, then realize, and not lift a finger to prevent such exclusion! It's hardly human . . . I wonder if that Olga has a heart."

"Who's to say she isn't suffering?"

Lily put down her sewing, her needle stuck through the thick fold of cloth; she hadn't thought of this. Her eyes immediately filled with tears.

"Have we made her unhappy?"

"I think she was unhappy when she got here and she's even unhappier now."

"Poor woman! And it's our fault . . ."

"I think, above all, that we can count on her."

"Yes, you're right," exclaimed Lily, drying her tears with her sleeve. "Let's confide in her now, quickly. It hurts me too much to think that she's just a prisoner like the rest of us and we're making her troubles worse by making life impossible for her."

After a few minutes of consultation, the women decided they would risk unveiling their plan, and Tatyana would take the initiative.

After that, the camp lapsed again into its drowsiness; outside, the frost was extreme; a few furtive squirrels scrabbled across the snow among the huts.

With her left hand Olga was crumbling an old crust of bread; with the other she was holding her empty dish.

Tatyana came over.

"Did you know that you're allowed a pack of cigarettes every two days?"

"Has it occurred to you that I have noticed and that I've been smoking?"

Olga's words had sprung from her mouth sharply, precipitously; the sudden cessation of a week of silence accelerated her elocution.

Tatyana noticed that despite her aggressive tone, Olga had spoken more than usual. She must be missing human contact . . . so Tatyana reckoned it was all right to continue.

"Since you notice everything, you will have seen no doubt

that none of us smokes. Or that we only smoke now and again when the guards are around."

"Uh . . . yes. No. What do you mean?"

"Haven't you wondered what we use our cigarettes for?"

"Oh, I see; you swap them. You use them for cash in the camp. You want to sell me some? I don't have anything to pay with . . ."

"You're mistaken."

"So if you don't pay with money, what do you pay with?"

Olga looked at Tatyana with a suspicious scowl, as if she knew ahead of time that whatever she was about to discover would disgust her. So Tatyana took her time to reply:

"We don't sell our cigarettes, we don't swap them either. We use them for something other than smoking."

Because she sensed she had piqued Olga's curiosity, Tatyana broke off the discussion, well aware that she would have a stronger case if the other woman had to come back to her to find out the rest.

That very evening, Olga went over to Tatyana and looked at her for a long time, as if to ask her to break the silence. In vain. Tatyana repaid her in kind for the first evening.

Olga eventually capitulated: "Right, what do you do with the cigarettes?"

Tatyana turned to her with a searching look.

"Did you leave people you love behind?"

Olga's only reply was a fleeting, pained expression.

"So did we," continued Tatyana, "we miss our men, but why should we be more worried for their sake than for our own? They're in another camp. No, what really hurts, is the children . . ."

Tatyana's voice faltered: the image of her two daughters had just pricked her conscience. Out of compassion, Olga placed her hand on Tatyana's shoulder: a sturdy, powerful hand, not unlike a man's.

"I understand, Tatyana. I have also left a daughter behind. Fortunately, she's twenty-one."

"My girls are eight and ten . . ."

It took all her remaining strength to keep from crying. Besides, what more was there to add?

Brusquely, Olga pulled Tatyana against her shoulder and Tatyana—tough Tatyana, the network leader, the eternal rebel—because she had found someone tougher than herself, she wept for a moment against a stranger's chest.

Safely unburdened of her surfeit of emotion, she picked up the thread of her thoughts.

"This is what we use the cigarettes for: we empty out the tobacco, and we keep the papers. Afterwards, by gluing the papers together, we can make a real sheet of paper. Here, come with me, I'll show you."

Tatyana lifted up a floor board and from a hiding place full of potatoes she removed a crackling pile of cigarette papers, where each joint, each glued crease thickened the delicate tissues, as if they were some millennial papyrus discovered in Siberia through some aberration of archeology.

She placed the sheets carefully on Olga's knees.

"There. One of us is bound to get out of here someday . . . and she'll take our messages with her."

"Fine."

"But you may have noticed, there's a problem."

"Yes, I can see that the pages are blank."

"Yes, blank on both sides. Because we don't have a pen or ink. I tried to write with my own blood, I stole a pin from Lily, but it fades too quickly . . . And besides, I don't scar well. Something to do with my platelets. Malnutrition. I don't want to go to the infirmary, it might make them suspicious."

"Why are you telling me this? What does it have to do with me?"

"Well, I suppose that you too would like to write to your daughter?"

Olga allowed a full minute of thickening silence to go by then says, gruffly, "Yes."

"So here's what we'll do: we'll provide you with the paper, and you get us the pencil."

"Now why would you think I have a pencil? That's the first thing they take off us when they arrest us. And we were all searched several times over before coming here."

"Your hair . . ."

Tatyana pointed to the thick halo of hair surrounding Olga's stern face. And went on staring at her.

"When I first saw you, I thought that . . ."

Olga interrupted her with her hand and, for the first time, she smiled.

"You are correct."

As Tatyana's eyes filled with wonder, Olga slipped her hand behind her ear, dug about in her curls and then, her eyes shining, she pulled out a thin pencil and handed it to her fellow prisoner.

"It's a deal."

It is no easy thing to measure the joy that warmed the women's hearts during the days that followed. Through that little pencil lead they had once again found their hearts, their ties with the world from before, a way to embrace their children. Captivity no longer seemed as arduous. Nor did guilt. For some of them did feel terrible remorse for the fact that they had put their political activities before their family life; now that they had been shipped off to the depths of the gulag, leaving their children at the mercy of a society they had despised and fought against, they could not help but regret their militancy and suspect that they had failed in their duty, and thus proven themselves to be bad mothers. Would it not have been better simply to keep quiet, like so many other Soviet women, and immerse themselves in domestic values? To save their own skins, and the skins of their loved ones, rather than struggle to save everyone's?

While each of the prisoners had several sheets of paper, there was only one pencil. So after several meetings they agreed that each woman would have the right to three full sheets before all of the sheets were bound together in a stitched notebook which would be smuggled out at the first opportunity.

The second rule: each woman must write her pages without making any mistakes, in order not to waste the pencil lead.

While their decision was greeted with general enthusiasm that evening, the days that followed were more troublesome. Confronted with the obligation to concentrate all their thoughts onto three small sheets, each woman struggled: how to put together three essential pages, three testamentary pages that would imprint the essence of a life, that would pass on to their children their souls and their values, and convey for all eternity the significance of their time on earth?

The undertaking became a torture. Every evening sobs could be heard from the bunks. Some of the women couldn't sleep; others moaned in their dreams.

The moment they could seize a break in their forced labor, they would try to exchange their ideas.

"I'm going to tell my daughter why I am here and not with her. So that she'll understand, and maybe she'll forgive me."

"Three pages of guilty conscience to give yourself a clear conscience—do you really think that's a good idea?"

"I want to tell my daughter how I met her father, so that she'll know that she was born because of the love between us."

"Oh yes? And what if all she really cares about is finding out why you didn't stick around to love her."

"I want to tell my three daughters about their birth,

because each of their births was the most beautiful moment in my life."

"That's a bit short, no? You don't think they'll be sorry you restricted your memories to their arrival on the scene? You'd do better to talk about what came afterwards."

"I want to tell them what I would like to do for them."

"Hmm."

In the course of their discussions, they uncovered a singular detail: all of them had given birth to daughters. The coincidence amused them, then surprised them, to such a degree that they came to wonder whether the decision to incarcerate all the mothers of daughters together in ward 13 had not been deliberate on the part of the authorities.

But this diversion did not bring an end to their ordeal: what should they write?

Every evening Olga would wave the pencil and call out, "Who wants to begin?"

Every evening a diffuse silence would settle over the women. Time passed, perceptibly, like stalactites dripping from the ceiling of a cave. The women, heads down, waited for one of them to shout, "Me!" and to deliver them temporarily from their troubles but, after a few coughs and furtive glances, the most courageous would eventually say that they were still thinking.

"I've nearly got it . . . tomorrow perhaps."

"Yes, me too, I'm getting there, but I'm not quite sure . . ."

The days went by, whirling with snow flurries, crisp with immaculate frost. Although the prisoners had waited two years for the pencil, three months had already gone by and not one of them asked for the pencil or even accepted it.

So imagine their surprise when one Sunday, after Olga had lifted up the object and uttered the ritual words, Lily answered eagerly, "I'll have it, thanks."

They turned around, stunned, to look at plump, blonde

Lily, the most scatterbrained of them all, the most sentimental, the least headstrong—in short: the most normal. If someone had tried to forecast who among the prisoners would be first to start writing her three pages, Lily would surely have been placed among the stragglers. First would be Tatyana, or perhaps Olga, or even Irina—but sweet, ordinary Lily?

Tatyana could not help but stammer, "Lily . . . are you sure?"

"Yes, I think so."

"You're not going to . . . scribble, make a mistake . . . well, wear down the pencil?"

"No, I've had a good think: I'll manage without any mistakes."

Skeptical, Olga handed Lily the pencil. As she was giving it to her, she exchanged glances with Tatyana, who seemed to confirm that they were surely committing a blunder.

On the days that followed, the women in ward 13 stared at Lily every time she would go off on her own to write, sitting on the floor, alternating inspiration—eyes raised to the ceiling—and expiration, her shoulders curved to hide the marks she was making on the paper from the others.

On Wednesday she announced, satisfied, "I've finished. Who wants the pencil?"

A gloomy silence met her question.

"Who wants the pencil?"

Not a single woman dared look at another. Lily concluded, calmly, "Right, then I'll put it back in Olga's hair until tomorrow."

Olga merely grunted when Lily hid the object deep in her curls.

Anyone other than Lily—not as good, more aware of the complexities of the human heart—might have noticed that the women in the ward were now training jealous gazes upon her, perhaps even a touch of hatred. How had Lily, who really was close to being a moron, managed to succeed where the others had failed?

A week went by, and every evening provided another opportunity for the women to relive their defeat.

Finally, the following Wednesday at midnight, when the sound of breathing indicated that most of the women were fast asleep, Tatyana, tired of tossing and turning in her bunk, dragged herself silently over to Lily's bunk.

Lily smiled at her, gazing up at the dark ceiling.

"Lily, I beg you, can you tell me what you wrote?"

"Of course, Tatyana, would you like to read it?"

"Yes."

How would she manage? It was after curfew.

Tatyana huddled at the window. Beyond a spider's web was a field of pure snow, made blue by moonlight; if she twisted her neck, Tatyana could just make out the three small pages.

Lily drew near and asked, her tone that of a little girl who has done something naughty, "Well, what do you think?"

"Lily, you're a genius."

And Tatyana took Lily in her arms to kiss her several times over on her plump cheeks.

The next morning Tatyana asked two favors of Lily: permission to follow her example, and permission to share it with the other women.

Lily lowered her lashes, blushed as if she'd just been offered a bouquet of flowers, and chirped a few words which—though garbled, a sort of cooing in her throat—meant yes.

Epilogue

Moscow, December 2005.

Fifty years have passed since these events took place.

The man who is writing these lines is visiting Russia. The Soviet regime has fallen, and there are no more camps— although this in no way means that injustice is a thing of the past.

In the salons of the embassy of France I meet the artists who for years now have been putting on my plays.

Among them is a woman in her sixties who seizes my arm with a sort of affectionate familiarity, a mixture of brazenness and respect. Her smile glows with kindness. It is impossible to resist the mauve of her eyes . . . I follow her over to the window of the palace, with its view over the lights of Moscow.

"Would you like me to show you the most beautiful book in the world?"

"And here I was clinging to hopes of writing it myself, and you tell me I'm too late. What a blow! Are you sure of this? The most beautiful book in the world?"

"Yes. Other people might write beautiful books, but this one is the most beautiful."

We sit down on one of those oversized, worn sofas that must adorn the grand salons of embassies the world over.

She tells me about her mother, Lily, who spent several years in the gulag, and then about the women who shared that time with her, and finally the story of the book, just as I have related it above.

"I'm the one who owns the notebook. Because my mother was the first one to leave ward 13, she managed to sneak it out, sewn in her skirts. Mother has died, the others too. However, the daughters of the imprisoned comrades come to look at it from time to time: we have tea together and talk about our mothers, and then we read through it again. They've entrusted me with the task of looking after it. When I won't be here any-more, I don't know where it will go. Will a museum take it? I wonder. And yet it is the most beautiful book in the world. The book of our mothers."

She positions her face beneath my own, as if she were going to kiss me, and winks at me.

"Would you like to see it?"

We make an appointment.

The next day, I climb the enormous stairway leading to the apartment she shares with her sister and two cousins.

In the middle of the table, amidst the tea and sugar cookies, the book is waiting, a notebook of fragile sheets which the decades have left more brittle than ever.

My hostesses settle me into a worn armchair, and I begin to read the most beautiful book in the world, written by those who fought for freedom, rebels whom Stalin considered dan-gerous, the resistance fighters of ward 13, each of whom had written three sheets to her daughter, fearful that she might never see her again.

On every page there was a recipe.

POSTSCRIPT

This book came about when writing was forbidden to me.

A year ago, I was offered the opportunity to direct a film. As I had to work hard to prepare myself, to master the language of images, framing, sound, and editing, I had no opportunity to write. Later, the day before we were to shoot our first scene, I was handed a contract which forbade me from any skiing or violent sports; when I put my initials to it, I was also made to understand that it would also be preferable if I did no writing either, although, in any case, I wouldn't have the time.

That was too much of a provocation.

During the shooting and editing, therefore, I took advantage of the few rare hours when I had nothing to do in order to isolate myself from my crew; in the morning at breakfast, or in the evening in a hotel room, I sat at a table and wrote these short stories which I had been carrying around in my mind for a long time. This allowed me to rediscover the joy of clandestine writing, the one I'd known as an adolescent: filling the pages brought back an appetite for secret pleasures.

Ordinarily, short stories are made into films. Here, the contrary has occurred. Not only did my film allow me to write these short stories, but once it was finished—and once again to do just the opposite—I decided to adapt the original screenplay into a short story.

The film was called Odette Toulemonde, and the short story as well. However, anyone who is interested in both the cinema and literature, and who becomes acquainted with the two ver-

sions, will notice above all their differences, for I really did try to tell the same story using two languages, and unequal means: words in this case, and animated images on the screen.

August 15, 2006

ABOUT THE AUTHOR

Eric-Emmanuel Schmitt, playwright, novelist, and author of short stories, was awarded the French Academy's Grand Prix du Théâtre in 2001. He is one of Europe's most popular authors. His many novels and story collections include *The Woman with the Bouquet* (Europa Editions 2010) and *Concerto to the Memory of an Angel* (Europa Editions 2011).

Europa Editions publishes in the USA and in the UK. Not all titles are available in both countries. Availability of individual titles is indicated in the following list.

Carmine Abate

Between Two Seas
"A moving portrayal of generational continuity."
—*Kirkus Reviews*
224 pp • $14.95 • 978-1-933372-40-2 • Territories: World

The Homecoming Party
"A sincere novel that examines the bond between individual human feelings and age-old local traditions."
—*Famiglia Cristiana*
192 pp • $15.00 • 978-1-933372-83-9 • Territories: World

Milena Agus

From the Land of the Moon
"A jewel of a novel, it shines like a precious, exquisite gemstone."—
Libération
120 pp • $15.00 • 978-1-60945-001-4 • Territories: World except Australia & NZ

Salwa Al Neimi

The Proof of the Honey
"Al Neimi announces the end of a taboo in the Arab world: that of sex!"—*Reuters*
144 pp • $15.00 • 978-1-933372-68-6 • Territories: World except UK

Alberto Angela

A Day in the Life of Ancient Rome
"Fascinating and accessible."—*Il Giornale*
392 pp • $16.00 • 978-1-933372-71-6 • Territories: World

Jenn Ashworth
A Kind of Intimacy
"Evokes a damaged mind with the empathy and confidence of Ruth Rendell."—*The Times*
416 pp • $15.00 • 978-1-933372-86-0 • Territories: USA & Canada

Beryl Bainbridge
The Girl in the Polka Dot Dress
"Very gripping, very funny and deeply mysterious."
—*The Spectator*
176 pp • $15.00 • 978-1-60945-056-4 • Territories: USA

Muriel Barbery
The Elegance of the Hedgehog
"Gently satirical, exceptionally winning and inevitably bittersweet."—*The Washington Post*
336 pp • $15.00 • 978-1-933372-60-0 • Territories: World except UK & EU

Gourmet Rhapsody
"In the pages of this book, Barbery shows off her finest gift: lightness."—*La Repubblica*
176 pp • $15.00 • 978-1-933372-95-2 • Territories: World except UK & EU

Stefano Benni
Margherita Dolce Vita
"A modern fable...hilarious social commentary."—*People*
240 pp • $14.95 • 978-1-933372-20-4 • Territories: World

Timeskipper
"Benni again unveils his Italian brand of magical realism."
—*Library Journal*
400 pp • $16.95 • 978-1-933372-44-0 • Territories: World

Romano Bilenchi
The Chill
"Accomplishes what books three times its length seek to do."
—*Boston Pheonix*
120 pp • $15.00 • 978-1-933372-90-7 • Territories: World

Kazimierz Brandys
Rondo
"[Brandy's has] quickened the conscience and enriched
the writing of the twentieth century."—*Time*
400 pp • $16.00 • 978-1-60945-004-5 • Territories: World

Alina Bronsky
Broken Glass Park
"Bronsky writes with a gritty authenticity and unputdownable
propulsion."—*Vogue*
336 pp • $15.00 • 978-1-933372-96-9 • Territories: World

The Hottest Dishes of the Tartar Cuisine
"Utterly entertaining. Rosa is an unreliable narrator par
excellence."—*FAZ*
304 pp • $15.00 • 978-1-60945-006-9 • Territories: World

Massimo Carlotto
The Goodbye Kiss
"A masterpiece of Italian noir."—*Globe and Mail*
160 pp • $14.95 • 978-1-933372-05-1 • Territories: World

Death's Dark Abyss
"A remarkable study of corruption and redemption."
—*Kirkus* (starred review)
160 pp • $14.95 • 978-1-933372-18-1 • Territories: World

The Fugitive
"[Carlotto is] the reigning king of Mediterranean noir."
—*The Boston Phoenix*
176 pp • $14.95 • 978-1-933372-25-9 • Territories: World

Bandit Love
"*Bandit Love* is a gripping novel that can be read on different levels." —*Il Manifesto*
208 pp • $15.00 • 978-1-933372-80-8 • Territories: World

(with **Marco Videtta**)
Poisonville
"The business world as described by Carlotto and Videtta in *Poisonville* is frightening as hell."
—*La Repubblica*
224 pp • $15.00 • 978-1-933372-91-4 • Territories: World

Francisco Coloane
Tierra del Fuego
"Coloane is the Jack London of our times."—*Alvaro Mutis*
192 pp • $14.95 • 978-1-933372-63-1 • Territories: World

Rebecca Connell
The Art of Losing
"This confident debut is both a thriller and an emotional portrait of the long-term repercussions of infidelity."
—*Financial Times*
240 pp • $15.00 • 978-1-933372-78-5 • Territories: USA

Laurence Cossé
A Novel Bookstore
"An Agatha Christie-style mystery bolstered by a love story worthy of Madame de la Fayette . . ."—*Madame Figaro*
424 pp • $15.00 • 978-1-933372-82-2 • Territories: World

An Accident in August
"Cossé is a master of fine storytelling."—*La Repubblica*
208 pp • $15.00 • 978-1-60945-049-6 • Territories: World but not UK

Giancarlo De Cataldo
The Father and the Foreigner
"A slim but touching noir novel from one of Italy's best writers in the genre."—*Quaderni Noir*
144 pp • $15.00 • 978-1-933372-72-3 • Territories: World

Shashi Deshpande
The Dark Holds No Terrors
"[Deshpande is] an extremely talented storyteller."
—*Hindustan Times*
272 pp • $15.00 • 978-1-933372-67-9 • Territories: USA

Helmut Dubiel
Deep in the Brain: Living with Parkinson's Disease
"A book that begs reflection."—*Die Zeit*
144 pp • $15.00 • 978-1-933372-70-9 • Territories: World

Steve Erickson
Zeroville
"A funny, disturbing, daring and demanding novel—Erickson's best."—*The New York Times Book Review*
352 pp • $14.95 • 978-1-933372-39-6 • Territories: USA & Canada

Caryl Férey
Zulu
"Powerful and unflinching in its portrayal of evil both mindless and calculating."—*Publishers Weekly*
416 pp • $15.00 • 978-1-933372-88-4 • Territories: World except UK & EU

Elena Ferrante
The Days of Abandonment
"The raging, torrential voice of [this] author is something rare."—*The New York Times*
192 pp • $14.95 • 978-1-933372-00-6 • Territories: World

Troubling Love
"Ferrante's polished language belies the rawness of her imagery."—*The New Yorker*
144 pp • $14.95 • 978-1-933372-16-7 • Territories: World

The Lost Daughter
"So refined, almost translucent."—*The Boston Globe*
144 pp • $14.95 • 978-1-933372-42-6 • Territories: World

Linda Ferri
Cecilia
"A passionate and meticulous account of a young woman's search for her spiritual identity."—*La Repubblica*
288 pp • $15.00 • 978-1-933372-87-7 • Territories: World

Damon Galgut
In a Strange Room
"A taut, mesmerizing novel."—*New York Times*
224 pp • $15.00 • 978-1-60945-011-3 • Territories: USA

Jane Gardam
Old Filth
"Old Filth belongs in the Dickensian pantheon of memorable characters."—*The New York Times Book Review*
304 pp • $14.95 • 978-1-933372-13-6 • Territories: USA & Italy

The Queen of the Tambourine
"A truly superb and moving novel."—*The Boston Globe*
272 pp • $14.95 • 978-1-933372-36-5 • Territories: USA

The People on Privilege Hill
"Engrossing stories of hilarity and heartbreak."
—*Seattle Times*
208 pp • $15.95 • 978-1-933372-56-3 • Territories: USA

The Man in the Wooden Hat
"Here is a writer who delivers the world we live in…with memorable and moving skill."—*The Boston Globe*
240 pp • $15.00 • 978-1-933372-89-1 • Territories: USA

God on the Rocks
"A meticulously observed modern classic."
—*The Independent*
224 pp • $15.00 • 978-1-933372-76-1 • Territories: USA & Canada

Anna Gavalda
French Leave
"A comedy of happiness that will delight readers."
—*La Croix*
144 pp • $15.00 • 978-1-60945-005-2 • Territories: USA & Canada